SPY HIGH:
MISSION TWO

SPY HIGH:
MISSION TWO

CHAOS
RISING

A. J. BUTCHER

LITTLE, BROWN AND COMPANY
New York ·· Boston

FOR TONY JOYCE
THE SERIAL STORY STARTED IT

Little, Brown and Company

Time Warner Book Group
1271 Avenue of the Americas, New York, NY 10020
Visit our Web site at www.lb-teens.com

First U.S. Edition 2004
First published in Great Britain by Atom in 2003

Cover art by Jason Reed

Library of Congress Cataloging-in-Publication Data
Butcher, A. J.
[CHAOS connection]
CHAOS rising / A. J. Butcher. — 1st ed.
p. cm. — (Spy high ; #2)
Summary: Sequel to: The Frankenstein factory.
Originally published in Great Britain in 2003 under title: The CHAOS connection.
Summary: The members of the Bond team at Deveraux Academy, a special high school that trains students to be secret agents, try to save the world from a deadly computer virus designed by CHAOS to destroy computer programs and human life.
ISBN 0-316-73762-3 — ISBN 0-316-73765-8 (pbk.)
[1. Spies — Fiction.   2. High schools — Fiction.   3. Schools — Fiction.
4. Computer viruses — Fiction.   5. Interpersonal relations — Fiction.]   I. Title.
PZ7.B9684Sp 2003
[Fic] — dc21   2003053243

10   9   8   7   6   5   4   3   2   1

Q-FF

Printed in the United States of America

PART ONE

Sixty years from now, north of Boston, there's a school that's more than it seems.

People whisper the name of Deveraux Academy like a secret, and wonder what they've heard about. They know the school was founded by Jonathan Deveraux, one of the wealthiest men in the world, and that he is rumored to live on the premises but hasn't been seen in the flesh for fifteen years. They know that the school is so exclusive, so select, that not even the sons of presidents or the daughters of rock stars can get in. They know that the school's literature boasts of the "exceptionally talented," but exceptionally talented at what? Nothing more is revealed. Ultimately, all people really know about Deveraux Academy is where the school is located and what it looks like. But only from the outside.

You approach it through grounds the size of Rhode Island, mostly forest. If you're alert, you might notice the branches of the trees stirring, moving, even on breezeless days — keeping an arboreal eye on your progress. Because instead of bark or sap, the branches of the trees at Deveraux contain circuitry and sensors, carefully monitoring the presence of each and every trespasser on the school's property.

At last, the forest falls away, and you see the school itself ahead of you. It's as if the centuries have fallen away, too. Deveraux Academy is a sprawling, gothic fortress that seems perfect for hidden rooms and dungeons and screams in secret corridors. The kind of place where you wouldn't want the power to fail in the middle of the night and where you'd be inclined to wear a cross around your neck — and maybe even a few cloves of garlic for good measure.

Of course, you could stop there, if you didn't feel like going any farther, and watch Deveraux's students playing on the fields. There's always a football game going on. Always. And if you watch it long enough, you'll realize that it's the same plays repeated, over and over, like an endless rehearsal. And that realization might bother you, unless you already know that all you're observing are holograms designed to project an illusion of normality.

The true business of Deveraux Academy goes on inside.

Through the great oak doors that open automatically. Past the receptionist who, despite her pensionable age, could kill you in a dozen different ways with her bare and wrinkled hands. Past the phantom students forever on their way to classes that never start. Into one of the many book-lined studies, which, if you press the spine of the book that is not a book, proves to be not actually a study, either, but an elevator. An elevator that takes you down, beneath the ground, behind the facade, to the place where Deveraux Academy in many ways ceases to be, to a school that has been christened by its students with a different name.

Spy High.

There are uniforms here, but no blazers or ties or regulation-length skirts. At Spy High, students wear gleaming silver shock suits, and if you want to know why they're called that, try jumping someone wearing one in a dark alley: You're likely to find it an electrifying experience. There are classes here, too, but few that would be featured at other educational institutions — unless spycraft, history of espionage, advanced computer hacking, enemy-disabling techniques, and the handling of weapons of mass destruction suddenly become requirements of the curriculum. There is a hologym for all kinds of physical combat training, a virtual-reality chamber equipped with the latest cybercradles, and study and recreational facilities of every description.

And then there is the Hall of Heroes. A hushed location, this is a place for reverence and reflection. The plaque on the wall spells out its purpose in glittering golden letters: "Dedicated to the graduates of Deveraux Academy. To those who risk their lives for the sake of tomorrow." At the far end of the Hall, the Fallen are commemorated, those who have perished in the ceaseless battle between the forces of good and the agents of evil. Their holographic forms hover in beams of light, their names emblazoned below, as if they are sentinels standing still against the darkness of the world. If nothing else, they are a reminder to the students of Spy High that they haven't been chosen to play games, but to be active partipants in a deadly struggle that could cost them their very lives.

A group of students is entering the Hall of Heroes now. The tall blond boy leading the way is Ben Stanton, while the equally tall and equally blond girl whose hand he's holding is Lori Angel. They're what you might call *close*, and not just because, other than the obvious physiological differences between them, they look virtually identical. The rest of their team follows behind. The African-American girl, Cally Cross, with her dreadlocks impeccably in place as always, seems interested, her bright, intelligent eyes missing nothing. Jake Daly, who slouches along-side her, wears a bored expression beneath his tangle of black hair, but it would be a mistake to underestimate him. Look more closely, and you'll see that his dark, even swarthy, features and compact, muscular body exude power and intensity. He's some-one you'd want on your side in a fight. You might not think the same could be said of Eddie Nelligan, redhaired, looking like he's just gotten out of bed, grinning at some secret joke. But he's not here by accident, either. Then there's the last of the group, who's keeping a slight distance from the others, as if she doesn't quite belong: Jennifer Chen, green-eyed and lithe-limbed like a cat.

Ben directs his teammates to the far end of the Hall to the Fallen, where the memorials are of a more auspicious kind.

"Here they are," he breathes, as if referring to the saints, "the past winners of the Sherlock Shield."

Mounted on platforms like sculptures in a museum, the tro-phies immortalize each passing year's most successful student team at Spy High — those awarded the Sherlock Shield. The team members' faces, beaming, proud of their achievements, ro-tate slowly and three-dimensionally alongside their engraved names.

Ben, though, seems more interested in the platform at the end of the row, the one that, so far, lacks a trophy to be placed upon it. "And here's ours," he promises. "Here's where Bond Team's shield will go." His eyes sparkle as he imagines it, the honor, the glory — for the others as well as for himself, al-though as team leader, of course . . . "That's our target for this term. That's our goal. To win the Sherlock Shield." He turns to his teammates. "Anybody want to say different?"

Nobody does. Lori, always the dutiful girlfriend, squeezes his hand supportively. Jake Daly is less impressed, but from the terse nod of his head, he is no less committed. Cally says, "I'm with you," and Eddie says nothing, which the others assume means he's being serious for once. Jennifer's silence is also interpreted as agreement, allowing Ben to feel good about himself and inwardly applaud his idea of bringing Bond Team down to the Hall of Heroes.

But, in reality, Jennifer's silence denotes neither agreement nor disagreement, because she hasn't heard a word that has been said. The Sherlock Shield is of no interest to her whatsoever. Jennifer Chen has something else on her mind, something else entirely.

She knew she was dreaming. The smile on her face and the laugh in her throat kind of gave it away. She didn't do much of either these days. Besides, she was back home again, and Mom and Dad and little Shang were with her, and the light in the room was golden and without shadows. She was where she couldn't possibly be, with people who couldn't possibly be there, but Jennifer didn't care.

If only it could last forever.

She hugged her parents and her little brother, held them close, and it seemed as though she could feel them solidly against her own body, their hearts beating strongly in their chests. Which was impossible.

And the sound that she could hear was not the hearts of her family in any case, not even her own. It was the thumping of dull, hollow blows on the door. (Somehow the door was in the room, though Jennifer seemed to remember that it used to be at the end of the hall.) It was the flat, fatal beating on the door, like dirt being heaped on a coffin. And her parents heard it, too, and little Shang, and they knew what they had to do.

They turned to the door and the sudden darkness it held, gaping like a grave. They turned from Jennifer.

"No, don't go!" Her protests were useless. They went unheard. "Mom! Dad! Don't leave me!" The sound of the pounding filled the air.

Her parents were at the door. She couldn't see their faces.

"Don't let him in! Don't let him in!"

But they did. And night entered the room like the serpent in paradise. And though Jennifer clutched for her family with desperate fingers, she was too late. In her dreams, as in life, she was always too late.

At least she didn't wake up screaming anymore. Familiarity had provided her with some degree of self-control. She didn't want to disturb the others as she had done several times during last term — she still sensed Lori looking at her strangely, suspiciously from time to time. But she had to get up. Her bedside clock said 3 A.M. There was going to be no more sleep for her tonight.

Jennifer slipped out of bed and stole into the bathroom, locking the door softly behind her. Just in time. All of a sudden, the sobs came — deep, wracking groans of grief — and she fell to her knees by the toilet, knowing that she was going to be violently ill.

The trouble was, when it was over, she didn't feel any better.

And she hadn't forgotten what was imminent, either.

A cautious knocking at the door. "Jen? Are you all right in there?" Lori, practicing her nightly nurse routine. "I thought I heard . . . ?"

"No. I'm fine." She was surprised at how fluent the lie was, how strong her voice seemed. "Just a bit of an upset stomach, I think. I'll live." Bitterly.

The twisted part of her wanted to scream out, "Leave me alone! Go away! What do you know? What do you care?"

And in the mirror in the bathroom, Jennifer's face splintered into tears.

Routine. Daniel Daniels hated it.

Routine was turning him psychic. Daniel Daniels believed that he could now predict precisely what he'd be doing at any given point in the work day next week, next month, even next year, for the rest of his natural life. Routine was making a robot out of him as surely as if he'd had those cyberkinetic limbs that were all the rage these days. It was making him a cog in a machine.

If only something unusual would happen, a little bit of the unexpected.

But it was more likely that a meteorite would fall on his head.

Take this morning, for example (and Daniel Daniels wished someone would). Six o'clock: the alarm and his bed's automatic sheet-retraction service. Seven o'clock: Leave the house wearing the suit that might as well be a prison uniform, although it cost significantly more. Seven-thirty: Catch the hoverbus into the city, have to stand due to congestion problems that reduced the number of services. Eight-thirty: Arrive at the Wainwright Building where he'd worked for the past twenty years and was likely to have to work for the next twenty, no chance of parole.

Have his retina scanned for security purposes (though people were more likely to want to break out of the Wainwright Building rather than in). Be recognized by the doorman program and greeted with a cybersmile: "Good morning, Mr. Daniels. How are you today?" Plan one day on telling the doorman program exactly how he was feeling.

Enter the elevator. Watch Baines call out from across the marble foyer, "Hey, hold those doors!" Wait for him to slip inside. "Hey, nearly didn't make it today." Feel the desperate urge to punch him in the nose. Feel the very real need to scream as he says, "Gentlemen, which floors?" as if he hadn't been pressing those same buttons at the same time since the beginning of the world.

Walk with colleagues along the corridor of the seventieth floor, exchanging pleasantries and wishing they were dead. March with colleagues into separate offices, silent and civil, glass doors sealing them in with preset efficiency.

Start the day. Pray for it to end.

"Morning, Marilyn." At least Daniel Daniels didn't have to disguise the gloom in his voice for his computer. It responded to the vibration of his vocal chords, not his mood.

"Hello, Daniel," cooed the computer, activating itself obediently. "What would you like to do today? I'm always open to suggestions." Laughter tinkled from the screen as the face of Daniel Daniels's favorite movie icon of the last century winked coyly at him. The Marilyn Monroe program was one of the few things that made his day bearable.

"You'd better read me my e-mails first, Marilyn," he said, not that he expected anything exciting to be among them.

He was almost right.

"And one final message," Marilyn concluded several minutes later, "but it's not addressed to you personally, Daniel. It's not addressed to anyone by name. Should I still read it?"

"Sure, what does it say?" He was scarcely even curious. But for a strange second, Daniel Daniels was distracted. What was that he'd just heard? It came from another office close by. Had he just heard what he thought he'd heard? A scream?

"It's simply addressed to the World of Order," said Marilyn.

"Read it anyway." It couldn't have been a scream, but Daniel Daniels could see others standing in their own offices, all looking in the same direction and with equal puzzlement. Toward Baines's room. And was that Baines in there, hanging on the unyielding glass to be let out? Why would he be doing that?

Behind him, Marilyn giggled. "Oh, this is an odd one," she said. "I don't really understand it."

And now Harper, too, in the next office over. That look on his face, it was like sheer terror.

Behind Daniel Daniels, Marilyn continued to giggle, though her voice seemed lower now, darker and grating. He turned in time to see her face blister and blacken, as though it were being cremated. Her voice could no longer be heard. Something else was in the computer.

"Your time is over, little man," the something scowled. "The world you know, the World of Order, is coming to an end. Prepare to greet a new age, the Age of CHAOS."

"A virus," Daniel Daniels gasped to himself as a dark and terrible shape took form on the computer screen. "It's a virus."

Then his machine exploded.

It seemed to start a chain reaction: explosions bursting from one office after another, like an incendiary roll call. Daniel Daniels was thrown against the door by the detonation, but he was essentially unharmed. For a second, he even began to feel relief. Until the ceiling above him started to hiss and buckle and rupture, and cables spilled from it like black intestines. They snapped and swayed and sparked, and Daniel Daniels knew that if any of them so much as touched him, they'd be identifying him by his dental records down at the morgue.

The mechanism to release the door didn't work, of course. It was computer controlled. The virus had infected it, too. Manual operation was impossible. He was trapped. Daniel Daniels's colleagues had the same problem. Mad with panic, they were all screaming now, pounding on unbreakable glass as the murderous cables spilled into their cubicles, like snakes poised to strike.

An electric flash, blinding, white. An unusually high scream. A sizzling like charred steak. And Daniel Daniels's bulging eyes registered that Harper was no longer trying to escape. He wasn't the only one, either. The cables were striking with deadly accuracy — as though they, too, were under the virus's control. He saw poor Baines being throttled, gurgling his horror, and then yanked into the air, jerking like a puppet. And Daniel Daniels knew it would be his own turn soon. *What could he do?*

His chair. The glass. It was a chance. He seized it and swung — clumsily but with all the strength a man in the last minutes of life could muster — aiming it at the door.

Which slid open. As if all he really had to do was ask politely. The chair's momentum sent both it and Daniel Daniels spinning out of the office and sprawling humiliatingly on the floor. Daniel Daniels couldn't speak for the chair, but he didn't mind in the least. There was nobody else alive to see him, anyway.

He scrambled to his feet and scurried for the elevator. There were the doors ahead of him.

He was sobbing to himself. If somehow he could get out of this alive, if somehow he could survive, he'd never criticize routine again. He'd be happy to lead an ordered, regimented, preprogrammed life for the rest of his days. Happy? He'd be ecstatic.

The elevator doors saw him coming and opened obligingly.

The unusual? The unexpected? Daniel Daniels now hated them both.

He dived for the safety of the elevator, and maybe he'd been blinded by tears of relief, or maybe he didn't look, or maybe he didn't even care. But Daniel Daniels dived seventy floors straight down.

The elevator wasn't there.

"Final pair, take your positions," snapped Corporal Randolph Keene. "Ben Stanton and Simon Macey." He spat out their names like pieces of gristle, as though he harbored a personal grudge against them both.

Understandable enough in the case of Macey, Ben thought, *but Keene ought to be demonstrating a little more respect toward himself.* He'd soon be showing him why.

Ben and Simon approached the Wall, cheered on by their respective teammates. Ben could even hear Jake Daly whooping encouragement, any differences between them put aside (if not quite forgotten) for the duration of the competition. Bond Team versus Solo Team. Ben Stanton versus Simon Macey. It was always going to come down to this.

"Break a leg, Simon," Ben said.

"Break your neck, Stanton," came the response.

Ben grinned. For secret agents, emotions were bad. Emotions were baggage. They weighed you down, muddled your thoughts, got in the way between you and what had to be done. A secret agent had to repress emotions, eliminate them. Macey wasn't doing that. He was hating Ben instead of focusing on the Wall. It was a sure sign of defeat.

Ben sprayed the clingskin on the boots of his shock suit and liberally onto his hands. The clear, gelatinous substance encased his skin like a tight and invisible glove. Ben closed his fists and rubbed his palms together. He couldn't feel any stickiness at all, yet the clingskin was strong enough and adhesive enough to allow him to scale the Wall with no further artificial aid. "Look on it as a kind of human glue," they'd been taught.

"What are you ladies waiting for? An invitation to dance?" Keene repeated. "Take your positions before we all die of boredom."

They stood at the foot of the Wall, although what they had to climb wasn't really just a *wall*, of course. Most walls tend to be built from the ground up, for safety reasons if nothing else. The Wall, here in Training Chamber Two at Spy High, had been constructed from the roof (a long, long way above them, its lights like stars) and extended down, but it hadn't quite managed to reach the floor. The Wall hovered just above the boys' heads. It was sheer, and it glistened darkly.

"On your marks," barked Keene.

Ben tensed. Out of the corner of his eye, he saw Lori urging him on. She'd done her bit for the cause, winning her race against Solo Team's Sonia Dark. So had Jake and Cally. Only Eddie, predictably, and Jennifer, surprisingly, had lost.

"Set."

Like a spring, Ben told himself, crouching. *Be like a spring*.

So the score was three–two in Bond Team's favor. Only Ben and Macey were left. If Ben won, Bond Team won. If Ben won, Bond Team would take a vital advantage in the race for the Sherlock Shield. There was nothing else for it. He *had* to win.

"Go!"

Ben leaped, powering up with his legs. He slammed his hands against the smooth surface of the Wall and felt the clingskin holding him there effortlessly. He raised his feet to make contact with the Wall, even as the structure began to lean, began to move, slowly toppling, the angle to the floor gradually reducing from ninety degrees downward, increasing the pressure of gravity on those attempting to climb it. On the Wall, even when aided by clingskin, technique was everything.

Ben trusted his technique. He'd paid attention in class. He'd practiced hard. He thrust himself upward, higher, sliding his hands and feet over the slickness of the Wall's surface, never once breaking contact with it, spreading his fingers wide so that the clingskin could touch the maximum area possible. That was the trick. Press yourself as close to the Wall as to a girl you've always liked and never let go. Never give the clingskin a chance to stop doing its job. And focus, concentrate. Stick to your task, literally.

Ben slithered up the Wall.

It lowered to eighty-five degrees. Eighty. Macey was in hot pursuit. His leap had been as tall as Ben's, but he'd scrabbled a little with his feet. He was already behind. Ben took encouragement from this and reached up with his limbs perfectly synchronized. His heart raced. The roof was closer than the floor. *Seventy-five degrees . . . seventy . . .*

Ben felt gravity plucking at him, and for the first time, he felt a slight strain on the clingskin. If he wasn't careful, a hand or a foot could peel off the Wall like a bandage from flesh, and then he'd fall. Ben Stanton had not joined Spy High to fall.

Sixty-five degrees . . . sixty . . .

Was Macey gaining? How could that be? Macey was a loser, so obviously a loser that Ben half-expected it to be tattooed across his forehead. But he *was* gaining.

Fifty-five degrees . . .

He had to try something, confirm his advantage. Ben slanted sideways, cutting across what would have been Simon Macey's natural route up the Wall. It was like one car swerving in front of another, and just as the second car would have to brake unexpectedly hard in order to avoid an accident, so Simon Macey's upward rhythm was also interrupted.

"What the . . . ?" Macey drew his right hand from the Wall. It was enough. "No!" Gravity grabbed him and pulled.

Ben looked down with triumph in his eyes. "Not sticking around, Simon? Too bad."

Macey lashed out with his hand, clutching for Ben's leg. Didn't make it. With a howl of defeat, Simon Macey dropped from the Wall and plunged to the floor. He'd be all right, of course. The floor was softly padded to avoid physical injury.

The only part of Simon Macey that would be hurt would be his pride. Which was exactly how Ben liked it.

Fifty degrees . . . forty-five . . . But angles didn't matter now. Ben slickly, smoothly slid his way to the top of the Wall, hauled himself to the victor's platform, and raised his arms aloft. Below him, the little people cheered. He just hoped the cameras had been on.

Lori ran to Ben first, hugged and kissed him. The others didn't run, although they did walk kind of quickly, but they stopped short of a hug and a kiss, which, in the case of Jake and Eddie particularly, was only to be welcomed. There was a unanimous chorus of "good jobs" and other variations on the theme.

"You sure showed us failures how to do it," acknowledged Eddie, whose own effort at the Wall had been of the dangling, helpless variety.

"Well," said Ben, "somebody had to."

"With modesty, too," observed Jake ironically, nudging Jennifer. "What would we do without him?"

Jennifer replied with a vapid half-smile, making Jake frown. All right, so she'd also fallen from the Wall, but it just didn't seem as though that was the only thing troubling her. There was something else. Jake sensed it.

The students suddenly realized that Senior Tutor Elmore Grant had arrived.

"Were you watching us, sir?" Ben asked, clearly expecting an affirmative response supported by praise.

"No." Grant ran a hand through his hair. A bad sign. "I'm afraid I didn't see. . . ." *Who's dead?* Jake found himself wondering.

Whose parents have died? "I'm afraid I was watching . . . something else."

"Sir?" Cally said concernedly. "Is anything wrong?"

"I'd like you to come with me, Bond Team." Grant seemed to recover himself. "A situation has arisen."

"Situation, sir?" Ben was annoyed. *What could be more important than the celebration of their victory?*

"It's started," Grant said. "CHAOS is coming."

CHAPTER TWO

The room was screaming.

To be accurate, making noise was what Spy High's Intelligence Gathering Center did. The IGC was wired into every significant news network on the planet — as well as most of the insignificant ones — monitoring events across the globe as they happened, directly and immediately relaying the latest developments in human history to the school where Jonathan Deveraux and his team of tutors could decide what action, if any, the graduates of Spy High needed to take in order to protect and preserve the safety of mankind. Twenty-four hours a day, sometimes longer, the IGC echoed and re-echoed with the sound of a million voices in a thousand languages. The members of Bond Team were used to that. They expected it.

But they didn't expect the horrors that greeted them today.

Terror and trauma on every continent. Carnage and calamity from North Pole to South. Apocalyptic images like nightmares come true were blazing from the screens around them. A hovertel tossed from the skies and hitting the earth like a fireball. Computer-controlled traffic colliding and exploding. The solar cities of the California coast plunging into darkness. And on every screen, the same soundtrack to disaster: the whole world screaming. For once, no translation was necessary. Death has a common language.

"What's happening?" Cally stared, shocked at the screens. "It looks like the end of the world."

Lori slipped her hand into Ben's. Even though he didn't think to squeeze it reassuringly, it still felt better there.

"Sir?" A dismayed Jake turned to Grant.

"Keep watching," the tutor instructed.

"I can't," Jennifer protested, unusually squeamish. "This is too . . . turn it off! Stop it now!"

The screens went dead. A second of silence, almost as disturbing as the screams. Then on every screen, multiplied and menacing, a man in a mask like a photographic negative, the reverse of a human face, and Bond Team knew why they were here.

"We have spoken," announced the man, "and our words have been heard in destruction, disorder, and death throughout the world. Our language is CHAOS, a language your laughable so-called governments will soon come to understand more clearly than ever before. CHAOS: The Crusade for Havoc, Anarchy, and the Overthrow of Society. We are the enemies of your petty and repressive systems of order, your laws, and your institutions." The man in the mask leaned closer. "Your days are numbered. Law and order will be no more. It is time for CHAOS. We have spoken, and you have heard. We will be silent now for a while, so that you may consider what has been said, but we will return with our demands. And do not think that you can stop us. We can attack anyone, anywhere, and at any time. CHAOS is coming. And there is nothing you can do."

"I don't know. We can shut this guy up for starters, can't we?" Eddie looked across the room. "Where's the 'off' switch?"

"It doesn't matter," Grant said, as the IGC went silent, on its own accord, for the second time. "That was the entire communication. A little over an hour ago, it interrupted every major television broadcast worldwide. It seems this organization is claiming responsibility for the sequence of disasters you've just witnessed. Worse, it seems to be promising more."

"Then they've got to be stopped," Ben said, rather obviously.

"We've already reassigned all graduate teams to this one case," Grant said, "and we're trying to trace the source of their signal, so far without success. Whatever masking program they're using, it must be state of the art or beyond. What we need, and quickly, is a lead."

"Which is where you come in, Bond Team." The videoscreens were resurrected again. Now the grave, wise features of Jonathan Deveraux himself faced the six students, examining them steadily. "Your earlier encounter with a CHAOS agent may provide us with precisely the lead of which Senior Tutor Grant speaks."

Bond Team exchanged glances. As one, their minds drifted back to the past, to their last term. To their camping trip in the Wildscape. To their capture by Dr. Averill Frankenstein, the mad geneticist. And to their brief videoscreen dialogue with a similarly masked CHAOS agent.

It was rare for Deveraux to be seen by Spy High's students, and even when he was, it was only through a videoscreen. But for the founder to ask for help as explicitly as he was doing now was unprecedented. If they could only make a contribution toward the defeat of CHAOS, Ben thought, there'd need to be a special place in the Hall of Heroes set aside just for them, with himself, as team leader, tastefully prominent. But sadly, not even he dared to tell Deveraux anything but the discouraging truth: "I don't think there is anything, sir. We were fully debriefed after the event. . . ."

"I am aware of that, Stanton," said Deveraux. "I have the tapes."

"Of course, sir." Ben sounded embarrassed. "I only meant that I can't think of anything else."

"Were you not helpless in Frankenstein's gene chamber for much of the time? Perhaps some of your teammates have more to contribute."

"Actually, sir," said Cally, feeling that Deveraux was being a little unfair, "I doubt we can add any more than Ben. The agent we saw said exactly the same kind of things as this one today. It could even be the same man, what with the mask and every-thing."

Deveraux uttered a disappointed sigh. With it, Ben's special place in the Hall of Heroes seemed to vanish. "Very well. But if anything does occur to you, to any of you, no matter how slight or inconsequential it might seem to be, bring it to the attention of Senior Tutor Grant at once. We must explore every possible outcome in this present crisis. We cannot rest until the threat of CHAOS is over."

Deveraux blinked out.

Stung by the founder's implicit criticism, Ben took charge. "Meeting," he hissed conspiratorially to the others. "The girls' room. In an hour. Before Weapons Instruction. Let's go through the Frankenstein business again, just in case." He was pleased to see the general nods of agreement. "Everyone be there, okay? *Everyone.*"

That was clear enough, Ben thought. *Time. Place. Purpose.* So it was a bit of a shock for him when Bond Team reconvened with one member short, and it was the last person he would have ex-pected to be missing.

"Where's Lori?" he asked.

* * *

She sat in the rec room, but she could have been anywhere. Her eyes were open, but they weren't seeing her immediate environment.

Inside her head, Lori was back in Frankenstein's gene chamber.

She shuddered as she relived her ordeal. Pounding on unyielding glass. Trapped like a specimen in a jar. The gene gas itself, lapping at her ankles, rising to her knees, her thighs, a gray tide dragging at her helpless limbs. Tasting it, bitter and acrid in her mouth, when her lips had been pried open by the need to breathe. And worst of all, feeling it working on her, reshaping her, molding something new from the inside out, feeling herself drifting, her identity and her humanity drowning.

Lori squeezed her eyes shut, as if memories could be denied that way. Maybe some could, but not this one. The gene chamber was always going to be with her, a constant and chilling reminder of her own mortality.

She'd told Ben how she felt, of course. He'd been appropriately sympathetic — all concerned expressions, soothing hands, and calming kisses, but it was clear he hadn't really understood. And this from someone who'd been trapped alongside her in the gene chamber, who'd tasted the transforming gas with her. The experience hadn't seemed to have affected Ben, or if it had, he wasn't letting on. "But it's all right now, babe. It's all done with," he'd said. "We survived." Which was true. "The gene chamber's been destroyed." Also true. "You can forget about it now." Well, two out of three wasn't bad.

But she didn't want to go over it all again. Let the others meet up and discuss it if they wanted to. She'd make her excuses to Ben sometime later. For now, all she wanted to do was sit here quietly and not be disturbed.

Somebody else had other ideas.

"Vanessa? Vanessa, how charming of you to come."

To begin with, Lori didn't respond largely because her name was not Vanessa. But it was hard to remain oblivious when Gadge Newbolt plumped himself down in front of her, beaming as if he were meeting an old friend for the first time in years.

Gadge Newbolt, or Professor Henry Newbolt to be more accurate, had been the scientific genius behind virtually all of Spy High's technological marvels, hence his nickname: "Gadge" as in "gadget."

"Vanessa," he crooned again. Lori glanced behind her. No Vanessa here. "My dear."

Unfortunately, Newbolt's brilliant brain had burned out long ago, and his famous gray cells were heaped in his skull like ashes. Now he was little more than an old man in a white coat, allowed to wander the school's corridors at will as a kind of merciful reward for all he'd contributed in the past. Before he went senile.

Nowadays, though, Gadge tended only to talk to walls, not people. And he'd never before now, to Lori's knowledge, called anyone Vanessa.

"Professor Newbolt," she addressed him nervously, wondering where the "my dear" had come from. She'd been warned about old men in white coats.

"Professor . . . ? No, my dear," old Gadge laughed, "what happened to "Grandfather"? Call me Grandfather like you always used to."

Oops. Ben's meeting suddenly seemed quite important, after all. "Nice to see you, Professor, but I've got to be . . ." Lori stood, smiling falsely. And saw the hurt in the old man's eyes. His thin lips quivered.

"Don't go, Vanessa," he said. "Not so soon. Not again. You've only just arrived, and you haven't been to see your old grandfather for such a long time."

"Professor, I'm not Vanessa." Lori's first thought was to set Gadge straight. But then his brow furrowed, and she realized it would probably cause less harm if she pretended and played along with his delusions.

"Vanessa?" A final plaintive plea.

"Yes, Grandfather?" she tried.

Gadge brightened again immediately, grasped her hands in his, and shook them as Lori resumed her seat. "Oh, it is good to see you, my dear. It's been too long. Your old grandfather was beginning to wonder whether you'd forgotten him."

May be some truth in there, Lori thought. She was determined to find out more about Gadge's past if she could. But for now: "Oh, no, I've been busy, that's all. Of course I'd never forget you."

"Vanessa, Vanessa." Gadge dabbed fat, wet tears from his eyes. "You always were a good girl. And I've been busy, too, very busy indeed. Come and see what your old grandfather has been doing. See what I've got to show you in my lab."

Now this was probably going too far. Gadge had hopped to his feet and was tugging eagerly at Lori's arm, and she knew she'd have to make an excuse now. Lessons resumed in a few minutes, and it wasn't a good idea to skip them. Miss a class at Spy High, and you could miss something that could save your life one day. She'd have to leave. But then Gadge let go of her anyway. His hands fluttered in the air like falling leaves.

"Vanessa?" he said pathetically. "Where is my lab? I can't seem to . . . where is it?" He was like a child parted from its parents in a vast and terrifying public place. "Vanessa, can you help me? Please help me. Take me to my lab."

Lori sighed. How could she refuse? She'd have to catch up on her Weapons Instruction later.

"It's all right," she said, taking the old man's hand. "Let's go to your lab, Grandfather."

"Grandfather?" If Ben's jaw dropped any lower, Lori would be able to inspect his tonsils from the other side of the room. "You actually called him *Grandfather*?"

"Well, yes, I didn't see why not, Ben, what else could I do?" She looked for support from Cally, who seemed eager to provide it by repeating her last words and nodding a lot — "That's right, what else could she do?" — and from Jennifer, who was sitting, glazed, on her bed and not registering any interest in the real world whatsoever.

"What else?" Ben wasn't convinced. "You could have suggested that the old man get some therapy and then joined us at Lacey Bannon's Weapons Instruction lesson, that's what else." Sometimes he just didn't understand Lori. Where was her sense of duty? If only everyone was more like himself.

"Oh, Ben," Lori sighed exasperatedly. "It wasn't as easy as that. You didn't see what poor Gadge was like. You weren't there."

"That's right," Cally echoed. "You weren't there."

"Sounds like Gadge wasn't all there, either," snorted Ben unsympathetically. "So what happened next? It doesn't take an hour to get from Gadge's lab to the weapons chambers. Take a diversion to help some old ladies across the street, Lori?"

"It's that caring attitude that makes me love you, Ben," she replied. "Actually, I couldn't get away at once. Gadge was so pleased that I was there. He wouldn't let me leave. He was like a little kid showing an adult his toys. Showed me all his latest inventions."

"I thought he wasn't supposed to have invented anything worthwhile for years."

"They were just boxes with wires poking out of them, some old batteries, circuits, and lights. Nothing. Junk. And yet, he believed they were something wonderful. He wanted me to admire them. So I did. It was all so sad, really."

"You're telling me. Humoring a senile old fool when you should have been with the rest of us learning something useful."

Lori laughed ironically. "What? How to kill people in interesting new ways?"

"Listen," Ben reprimanded, "when we're out on a mission, you're going to find a laser cannon a bit more of an asset than a cozy bedside manner. I doubt you're going to get too far with these CHAOS goons by calling them grandfather and smiling at them sweetly. Know what I mean?"

"Actually, I do know what you mean," Lori said, "which is why I left Gadge's lab as soon as I could. After a while, he became so absorbed in all his tinkering that he seemed to forget I was even there. Then as I was creeping out, he noticed me again, but he didn't call me Vanessa or anything. Didn't seem to recognize me at all. Just said this was a private lab and students weren't allowed. His mind had obviously wandered off again, so

I did, too. Only by then, Weapons Instruction was already over. Dare I ask if I missed anything important?"

"I'm afraid you did," Ben said officiously. "Lacey introduced us to the latest version of the stasis rifle with infrared sights for shooting in the dark."

"Yeah? Well, I hope you'll be very happy together."

"Very funny," he grunted. Cally certainly seemed to think so. "Let's hope you find things just as amusing in the Gun Run next week. Stasis rifles are included, and this one counts for the Shield. Or maybe you think winning that is a joke as well now, Lori. And maybe I'll just leave you to it." How had his day come to this? It had started so well with the Wall, but since then, it had fallen apart. First Deveraux, now Lori. Frowning petulantly, Ben turned to go.

"Ben, I didn't —" Lori called after him.

The door slammed.

"Have you ever thought about trading him in for a more mature model?" Cally wondered aloud.

"I don't think I could." Lori blushed. "I don't think I'd want to. I know he can be difficult at times, and short with people, and intolerant, and a bit selfish . . ."

"Sorry, Lori," interrupted Cally, "but are you Ben's girlfriend or his analyst?"

"Only you should see him when we're alone." Lori blushed again, proudly. "Then you'd see a different Ben, a better Ben. He can be so gentle, so . . ."

"Yeah, well we don't want to go there, do we?" Cally laughed. "We'll take your word for it, won't we, Jen?"

"Anyway, I think I'd better . . ." Lori gestured after Ben. "I'd better apologize. Ben was right, really. I shouldn't have missed the lesson."

"What? No way." Cally shook her head in mock disbelief. "He stormed out. You go after him now, and we're talking personal humiliation. The way he spoke to you — let him come crawling back and apologize, Lori, assuming Ben Stanton's even physically capable of saying sorry. Let him know who's boss. That's what we'd do, isn't it, Jen?"

Cally and Lori both seemed to realize at the same time that Jennifer was not quite with them.

"Jennifer? Hello? Jen?"

IGC DATA FILE FBA 8320

"Men like Boromov Corbin and Pascal Z see technology as a means of reinforcing the divide between the rich and the poor, the haves and the have-nots of the world. They talk about technoimperialism, about the technologically advanced nations exploiting those countries that lack an industrial or scientific base. At the same time, this CHAOS organization seems to be going even further, disrupting technology as a way of destabilizing society itself. It seems clear to me that our entire way of life is facing a major crisis." Professor Talbot went on to say . . .

She didn't sleep the entire night. She didn't dare. To close her eyes would be to dream, and to dream, on this night more than any other night in the year, would be to invite the shadows in, to leave her defenseless before the tall, dark man — the man in the doorway.

So Jennifer lay on her back with her arms at her sides, as if she was practicing death, and stared at the ceiling as if it were the lid of a coffin.

And maybe she'd already surrendered. Maybe she'd fallen asleep without realizing it. With the room so black, it was difficult to tell for sure whether her eyes were open or closed. She thought she must be asleep because the doorway was suddenly before her with the man's shape in it. But perhaps she was still awake, and the man who chuckled like the rattle of a cobra was no longer content to remain in her dreams, in her past, but was emerging into the here and now to claim her. On this day of all days, that would be apt.

It was the anniversary of the day he'd claimed her parents.

Jennifer whimpered softly in her throat, twisted the sheets in her hands, and longed for daylight.

"You all right, Jen?" Jake asked at breakfast, trying to look behind her eyes to where the truth might lie. "I don't want to sound intrusive, but you look like you've seen a ghost."

"Could be worse," joked Ben. "Could have seen Eddie in the shower."

"Oh, very funny," Eddie huffed. "On the other hand, though, Jen, if you ever wanted to see me in the shower, I'm sure something could be arranged. You know, you could scrub my back . . ."

"You're better off scrubbing the whole idea," said Jake, a note of warning beneath the humor. "If you know what I mean."

"I'm fine, anyway," said Jennifer, not meeting anybody's eye. "Just let it go."

But Jake wasn't satisfied. If only Jennifer would allow him to get closer. He wanted to, she knew that, but still she kept shutting him out, as if there were a closed door between them that she didn't dare open. He decided to try again after martial arts, and if that didn't work, he'd keep on trying. Jake Daly didn't give up easily.

Today's lesson was kendo, the way of the sword. Not steel swords with killing blades, of course, but the *shinai*, the bamboo blade.

Bond Team prepared themselves. They donned the protective armor, adjusting and tightening the breastplates, tugging on the padded gloves, and hiding their faces behind the *men*, the face masks with steel grills.

Like bars, Jennifer found her blurred brain thinking as she fixed her *men* into place. Bars to imprison her, bars to suffocate her. She felt her breathing quicken, as though she'd been running a great distance and was about to collapse. But it wasn't just the grill that was confusing her, her sight was thick and muddy, too — nothing seemed clear around her. It was the lack of sleep, she realized, over many nights. She couldn't cope with it. And especially today, on the anniversary.

Mr. Korita, who like Bond Team was fully regaled in his *dogu* armor, drew them together and talked about the lesson. Jennifer wasn't following what he was saying. She glanced from side to side. Everybody looked the same, concealed with secret faces behind the bars. She couldn't tell who they were anymore. She couldn't even tell who she was.

Mr. Korita had said something. And then they were selecting their *shinai*. The sword felt good in her gloved hands, strong, true, something to rely on.

Her mind whispered a memory. *"Mom! Dad! Don't leave me!"*

And she suddenly realized the masked people surrounding

her were laughing. And they were backing away from her, leaving her alone in the center of the gym with the little man who gave orders.

He was giving orders to her. His sword was raised in front of him. He wanted to fight her. She knew that she had to fight him and raised her own *shinai* accordingly. She wondered who he was.

Then he was at her, like lightning. Before she could even move to defend herself, striking at both sides of her torso, the impact of each blow dulled by her armor but felt nonetheless. And then, with an expert and almost invisible twist of his *shinai*, he severed hers from her hand and sent it skittering across the floor.

Jennifer sensed the loss and scrambled after her sword.

The others were laughing at her. Or were they? Or was it just the thudding of blood in her ears? The pounding of fist on door. She groped for her weapon. On her knees, she clutched its handle and crouched.

Toward her approached a man in a mask, wielding a weapon.

And she knew who it was. She suddenly knew. It was him, the night man, the man in the doorway. He'd come for her at last. But he couldn't have her. He wouldn't take her. She was not weak, not like her parents. She'd made herself strong. She'd show him exactly how strong. She'd show them all.

A cry of rage and hurt and fury tore from her throat as Jennifer leapt to her feet. Her body shook with anger and hate.

Show him? She'd kill him.

CHAPTER THREE

It hadn't been a good idea for Jennifer to be the one to face Mr. Korita. Jake had known that from the start. Not today, not when she was behaving so strangely. But somehow it had happened anyway. It was as if their teacher was able to sniff out individual weaknesses like a bad smell, hone in on them, and exploit them ruthlessly. Jake supposed that that was what he was paid to do, to keep them on their toes. After all, you couldn't afford a bad day as a secret agent. A bad day could get you killed.

Speaking of which . . .

He thought that as soon as Jennifer was disarmed that would be the end of it. Game over. He was wrong. Suddenly, Jennifer sprung to her feet again, propelling herself toward their teacher and swinging her *shinai* directly at his head. Even Mr. Korita seemed surprised. For a second, he paused. For less than a second. Then he whipped up his own *shinai* to block Jennifer's blow. The crack of bamboo made Bond Team flinch.

Jennifer was not deterred. She struck down at his side, savagely, intending harm. Mr. Korita blocked again. She whirled and aimed at his back, her *shinai* slicing open wounds in the air. Mr. Korita pivoted so that the flailing sword missed him, though not by much. He tried to move to the offensive himself, but recklessly, relentlessly, Jennifer lashed blows at him, heedless of her own safety, forcing block after desperate block, pushing the teacher back.

"She's doing really well," Ben approved.

"No, this isn't good." Jake saw his anxiety reflected in Cally and Lori. "She's lost it or something. This is for real."

"What do you mean?" Eddie was with Ben. "This is great. Sure Jen's last name isn't Lee?"

"Shut up, Eddie," snapped Jake. "Open your eyes. This has got to be stopped before someone gets hurt."

Mr. Korita seemed to share a similar sentiment. They heard him call *"Yame!"* (stop) and *"Shobu-ari"* (end of contest), but Jennifer either couldn't hear or wasn't listening. Her whirling assault continued, battering the teacher's *shinai*, threatening to overwhelm him.

Mr. Korita seemed to stumble and dropped to one knee.

Jennifer shouted in triumph, lifted her weapon high like an executioner's ax. Her victim's head was bowing before her.

"Jen, no!" Jake cried.

The teacher's *shinai* stabbed out, ramming Jennifer's abdomen. The blow drove home, through her armor, like a dagger in her guts. All of a sudden, the spell was over. Jennifer was clutching at her stomach, gasping, doubling up, keeling over, her weapon clattering to the floor. Then she was on her knees, retching and shuddering, and Mr. Korita was beside her, loosening the cords of her mask, removing it. Her black hair spilled like ink.

"I'm sorry," she panted. "I'm so sorry."

"Not now," calmed Mr. Korita. "Just breathe. Slowly, deeply. You're all right."

No, thought Jake, as Bond Team closed ranks around their fallen comrade, *she isn't.*

He was still thinking the same later as he stood banging on

her door, knowing that she was inside, demanding that she talk to him. "Jennifer! Jen! You can't keep this door locked forever. You've got to come out sometime. Listen, I don't know what the matter is, but silence won't fix it. Let me help you. Let me in."

Inside, curled like a fetus on her bed, Jennifer heard Jake's pleas but did not respond. Dared not. She had to be strong, for herself, for her parents. She'd been weak today in Korita's class, had let the anniversary take over and cloud her judgment, betray her inner rage. She couldn't allow that to happen again. She wouldn't.

Stone cold. That was what she had to be. Learn from Spy High, and wait for the moment that would inevitably come for real, not in dreams.

Yet something in Jake's voice was tempting. "I want to help Jennifer, that's all." She could take refuge in that. But to rely on someone else was to be vulnerable to someone else, and vulnerability was weakness. Besides, how could Jake help her? To help you had to understand, and how could Jake possibly understand?

But when the knocking stopped and with a sigh Jake's voice drifted away, Jennifer did not feel better. It shocked her to realize that she felt worse.

"Well how much longer is he going to be?" Ben complained, tapping his watch for no apparent reason. "We'll all have graduated before Daly gets here at this rate. I say we start now, and Jake'll just have to play catch up."

"We can't do that, Ben," said Cally. "Jake's gone to see whether he can get any sense out of Jennifer, and seeing as she's the subject of our little gathering — our little gathering behind her back, if I might stress that small fact — then I think we need to wait for him."

"You think that, do you?" said Ben. Other than Jennifer and Jake, the other members of Bond Team were grouped around a table in the quietest corner of the rec room. "Who else thinks that?"

"Probably all of us, O leader," said Eddie, pointing toward the door, "here he comes now."

"Are you all right, Jake?" asked Lori as their teammate slumped into a seat alongside them. "Did you talk to Jennifer?"

"Through the door," Jake said, "which she wouldn't open." He shrugged with a dejected helplessness. "I don't know what to do."

"Well, that's why we're here, isn't it?" Ben pressed. "To decide what to do."

"That's why *you* called us here, Ben," corrected Cally, "though I'm not sure it's our place to *decide,* as you so cheerfully put it, about Jen or anybody else on the team."

"Say that again on a mission," Ben responded, "when Jennifer loses it big time, like she did this morning and puts everyone's lives in jeopardy."

"Yeah, it'd make me feel a lot better in my final moments to have you whispering 'I told you so' in my ear, Benny boy." Eddie smiled thinly.

"The point is," Cally frowned, "that we're not on a mission yet, and we're not going to be on one for another eighteen months at least. The point is that we're still training, and part of the purpose of training is to identify and rectify any areas of weakness that any of us might have. Even you, Ben. See, I don't really understand why we're having this little meeting at all. Jennifer's got something she just needs to work out, that's all."

"That's not all," denied Ben, "and you know it, Cally. She went wild in a normal, routine martial-arts lesson. No extra psychological pressure, nothing. And there she is, trying to smash Korita's head in. And I bet, if this was happening to certain other members of the team, you wouldn't be quite so vigorous in their support."

"What's that supposed to mean?" Cally's voice rose in anger.

"Seconds away, round one," contributed Eddie.

"Let's not get personal," intervened Lori. "Let's just calm down. Cally, Ben, nobody means anything. We're all on the same side, remember? We all want what's best for Jen."

"Good, Lori," Jake approved. "A sensible voice at last. And don't stop there. Say something else."

"Well," casting a slightly nervous glance toward her boyfriend, "I have to agree with Ben. Jennifer's actions today in the kendo . . . and it's not just today, either, is it? She's been increasingly, well . . . strange, self-absorbed, for a while now. I do think it's an issue."

"Well, if she wants lessons in developing a warm, winning personality," Eddie offered, "I'm always available. Very cheap rates."

"We want to help Jen, not doom her," Jake said. "Go on, Lori."

"Well, it seems to me we have a choice. Which is why Ben called us together here in the first place, isn't it?" Ben acknowledged Lori's correctness. "Cally's obviously right about our training, but none of the staff are with us all the time. Nobody here knows Jen as well as we do. We're her teammates, her friends. We can see there's a problem and the extent of it better than our teachers, even after today."

"Agreed so far," said Jake, and even Cally nodded, although reluctantly. "So the choice . . . ?"

"Is whether we try to deal with it among ourselves — support and help Jen within the team — or whether we report our concerns to Senior Tutor Grant."

"But anything could happen then," warned Cally. "She could even be booted from the school, and you know what that means: mind-wiped and returned home as if she'd never been here in the first place. No memory of us at all! I don't want that on my conscience. That's not an option."

"This isn't about your conscience, Cally," Ben contended, "and as far as I'm concerned, informing Grant is the only option. And don't look at me like that. I've got nothing against Jennifer personally. I like her as much as any of you. But the fact remains that if she's unstable —"

"Unstable?" Eddie queried. "How'd you get to that, Dr. Stanton?"

"All right, if she's *unpredictable* — better?" Ben rephrased. Eddie nodded. "If she's unpredictable, she could endanger us all. None of you can deny that." Four pairs of eyes increasingly cast downward suggested that Ben could be right. "Cally's point about not being on a mission yet, well, we weren't planning on getting involved with Frankenstein, were we? But we did. And who knows what might happen with CHAOS now? And even if nothing does, just our day-to-day lessons contain risks, don't they? This isn't exactly a normal school, is it? And don't we want to win the Sherlock Shield? We have to be able to rely on each other, and if Jennifer's going to be a liability, then —"

"All right, Ben," Jake interrupted. "That's enough. I think we know where you stand but you're not the only one here, and I think whatever we do has to be unanimous."

Everybody agreed, although not everybody seemed to like it.

Jake continued. "In the long term, Ben's got to be right, even though I don't like to admit it. There may come a time when the best thing for Jen will be some kind of professional help — counseling, I don't know what. But that time isn't yet, no way is it yet." Murmurs of agreement from three of the four listeners. "And I think it's our responsibility to help Jennifer through whatever's troubling her now, to give her our total support, and our loyalty, and our . . . friendship. And if we do that, then I think everything'll be fine, and that's what I'm voting for. What about the rest of you?"

"Absolutely," affirmed Cally.

"Yes. Yes." Lori piped in.

"Excuse me while I get my hanky, but yes. Agreed," Eddie said.

"It seems everybody's made their minds up. I won't rock the boat, but . . ." Ben began.

"It's all right," Eddie whispered to him. "There's always 'I told you so.'"

Ben caught up with Jake later, so it would be just the two of them. It meant that neither had to pretend to like the other. Already the brief sense of unity that the boys had shared during the Frankenstein episode seemed to belong to an unlikely past.

"You were very eloquent in there," Ben sneered. "Could almost forget you were a Domer."

"Your point? I don't want to keep you from your mirror."

"My point is what you didn't say, why you really want to keep Jennifer on the team." Ben was delighted to see Jake frown defensively. "Unrequited love is such a pain, isn't it? Well, maybe you'll get somewhere now. Jen's got to be grateful."

Jake regarded Ben with something close to contempt. "You really are low, aren't you, Stanton? If only Lori knew. . . ."

"Lori and me are for real," Ben returned. "We're a real couple. We hold hands in public and everything. What about you and Jennifer, hey, Jakey? And let me tell you, it's not going to be my girl that lets the team down, you understand me? And when that happens, Jake, when Jennifer flips again, it'll be your fault. Yours."

IGC DATA FILE FBA 8328

. . . latest in a series of raids on former associates and haunts of known technoterrorists. A government spokesperson said that the operation had been a success, recovering material of crucial significance in the hunt for CHAOS. The precise nature of the material was not disclosed for reasons of national security.

"You folks can sleep safely in your beds," the spokesperson declared. "Our boys are on the case, and nothing bad is gonna happen."

Rumors persist that the President, the Vice President, and the Joint Chiefs of Staff have already been moved to a secret underground base. . . .

CHAPTER FOUR

A normal day on a normal street, Lori reflected. That's what it looked like. A mother with her baby in a stroller. A group of friends laughing and joking on the corner. A young couple window-shopping, their backs to the world.

No traffic, though, neither parked or passing, which was unusual. And she herself didn't normally walk in the middle of the road. She didn't normally carry a stasis rifle, either.

But today was going to be something of an exception.

From nowhere and everywhere, a buzzer sounded. Lori tensed for action. It was her turn at the Gun Run. On screen in the control room, the others would be watching. The clock would be ticking. The honor of Bond Team was at stake.

The young couple turned to face her. Seemed they'd already made a pair of purchases. They were pointing them at Lori right now, taking aim, fingers on the trigger.

No trouble. Too slow. Lori was firing the stasis rifle almost before the threat was established. The stasis bolts jolted into the forms of her attackers. They snapped open silent mouths, jerked with contortions as a shimmering blue light rippled through them, finally stiffened, and fell. The paralysis effect of the stasis bolts was virtually immediate.

Which was just as well. Lori whirled in a new direction. The group of friends were no longer laughing and joking, no longer on the corner. They'd spread out across the street and were running toward her, blazing at her with shock pistols, the shells ripping at the road around her.

This was more challenging. Multiple targets and at a distance from each other. Her aim had to be flawless. Luckily for Lori it pretty much was. She eliminated the nearest assailant — always the first priority — the stasis bolts slamming him backward. Lori went down on one knee. Second priority: Make yourself a smaller target. She fired again and again, not wasting a single shot. They'd be cheering her in the control room, she knew. Ben would be working out whether her time was likely to be good enough to beat Simon Macey and Solo Team. *At this rate,* she thought, as her final attacker crashed to the ground, *he could start popping the champagne corks — if alcohol hadn't been banned at Spy High.*

Lori was on her feet again. The street was clear, but she couldn't take anything for granted. A telltale click to her left. The mother. The unexpected. Leaving the baby in the stroller while she fired a shock pistol at Lori's head. Lori dived forward, firing her own weapon as she did. The mother spasmed as the bolts shocked her system. Surely she was safe now, Lori thought.

But there was one final surprise. The killers on the Gun Run started early. Baby sat up. Baby was armed and dangerous in her carriage. It was a difficult shot, but Lori struck the forehead just beneath the bonnet.

The baby's mouth snapped open as the others' mouths had done and made an equal amount of silence. Because the baby, like the others, was a robot, part of the program.

Only Lori was real. Lori and the pressure of time.

She raced for the door at the end of the street. Her daylight Gun Run was over. Now she had to do it in the dark.

Through the door, it was suddenly night. Pitch black. Only

a faint, luminous glow on the floor, something like Spy High's answer to the Yellow Brick Road, showed Lori the way to go. This was no longer an environment where a successful secret agent wanted to rely solely on her own sight. Lori switched to radar vision, yanking the specially treated film from her belt and wrapping it around her eyes. It clicked into place. Now she had eyes not only in the back of her head but along its entire circumference. Lori was seeing the circle.

And just in time. A dangerous shape materialized behind her and to the right. Lori dropped to one knee again and fired the stasis rifle.

Missed. She frowned in disbelief. *Missed?*

She fired again. Got him, but not fatally. Her aim wasn't quite as sure in the dark, and the clock was ticking. With the third shot, her attacker fell, but behind her another two were approaching, already shooting at her. The air around her crackled and sparked.

Lori rolled over on the floor, stasis bolts stabbing at her assailants' legs. They went down, but she was wasting time, losing time. Her heart thudded an anxious warning. What had Ben said about the weapons instruction lesson she'd missed? (More enemies intruded between her and the way out.) "Lacey introduced us to the latest version of the stasis rifle . . ." (As she fired. And missed. And fired.) "With infrared sights for shooting in the dark." (And missed again.)

She didn't know how to do it. How did you activate the infrared sights?

Her assailants were advancing. They were taking aim. She'd given them too much time.

In the control room, they wouldn't be cheering now. Lori could imagine Ben's face. Aghast. And what had she said to him? "Yeah? Well, I hope you'll be very happy together." Maybe in the future, she'd better leave the sarcasm to Eddie.

Lori fumbled with her stasis rifle. It wasn't going to do her any good. She heard her attackers fire.

And she died. Ben was *not* going to be pleased.

She was right. He wasn't. It was nothing short of a miracle that Ben managed to restrain his fury with her for as long as he did, while the others commiserated and claimed that she was unlucky and that it wouldn't make any difference anyway in the long run — Bond Team was still too good to be beaten to the Shield by Macey and his crew. But Lori could tell from Ben's purpling face, like he were secretly being boiled, that he didn't entirely agree. "Can we talk, Lori?" he mumbled, hardly trusting himself to part his lips. "Just you and me. In an empty classroom, maybe."

When it came, Ben's eruption would have buried a town three times the size of Pompeii. "Who did you think you were playing against? Do you know what you've done, Lori?"

"I'm sorry, Ben." She hung her head in shame, knowing he was right.

"Sorry's just a word," Ben hurled back. "A word that losers use. And you know what, babe? You may have just single-handedly turned us into losers. Look at the scores now. Macey's team and us — neck and neck. Two events left. If you'd have pulled your weight in the Gun Run, we'd have been way ahead."

"I know it's my fault, Ben," Lori admitted abjectly. She

couldn't bear him glaring at her. She felt like a little girl being scolded. She remembered how frightened she used to be at a single harsh word from her father.

"You bet your baby blues it's your fault, Lo," Ben scolded. "That's why I'm mad. You were off Good Samaritaning with senile old Gadge when you should have been learning how to use the infrared sights with us. You clearly didn't bother to catch up on your own time, so you get frazzled on your Gun Run and cost us vital points."

"Ben . . . please . . ." But Lori couldn't deny any of it.

"So what's going on, Lori? You on Simon Macey's side now, is that it?"

"No, of course not." Lori was shocked. "How can you say that? How can you even think . . . ?" She put her arms out to Ben.

He stepped backward with disdain, like a rich man to a beggar. "I don't want to touch you right now, Lori," he said coldly. "Right now, I'm not even sure I want to look at you. You've let me down, you realize that? I can't . . ." A look of genuine pain scarred Ben's features. "You've let me down."

He turned on his heel and stalked out of the room. His anger must have made him deaf. He didn't respond to a single one of Lori's pleas for him to stay and for them to talk it through. His rage must have blinded him, too. He never noticed Simon Macey lurking outside the classroom, greedily devouring every syllable that had passed between him and Lori.

Simon smiled to himself and nodded knowingly. He gazed at an unhappy Lori through the glass of the classroom door. And planned.

IGC DATA FILE FBA 8330

. . . unexpected consumer boom in the wake of the CHAOS atrocities.

"What's the point of saving for a rainy day now?" demanded one fran-
tic shopper. "If CHAOS has its way, there probably aren't many days left. Me,
I'm going to have a heck of a good time before the lights go out."

Jennifer crouched in the bushes close to the athletics track and
watched Jake running. He'd already completed several laps, his
jersey hanging with increasing dampness from him, but he
didn't look like he was anywhere near ready to stop. His expression was stony and set, his limbs on automatic. He was chasing
something that he couldn't catch.

Part of Jennifer enjoyed her secret spectatorship, admired
the strength of Jake's body, the power of his pounding legs. Part
of her. Another part wondered what on earth she was doing,
sneaking around in the bushes like some sort of Peeping Tom.
Why wasn't she in the hologym if she was feeling a little more
balanced again, practicing her kendo, her judo, her karate —
anything that would allow her to hit people on one of the combat programs? Or why, if she was feeling better, wasn't she apol-
ogizing to the others for her recent behavior?

Because Jake wasn't in the hologym, that was why, or with
the others. Jake was here. If only she could find the courage to
approach him.

It might have helped Jennifer if real people could sprout
thought balloons above their heads, like characters in comic
books. Then she'd have realized that there was only one subject
on Jake's mind, and that was her.

He'd thought maybe a good long run would relax him, or

help him find answers to the question of Jennifer Chen. Neither had happened. Why couldn't it be easy, Jake wondered? Why couldn't he have fallen for Cally when she'd revealed her feelings for him before Christmas? Or why couldn't Jennifer be as frank and as open as Lori? Why did not having a girlfriend, not having Jen, make him feel annoyingly inferior to Romeo Stanton? Basically, Jake mused mournfully, why wasn't he very good with girls?

The pitifulness of his position suddenly made him want to laugh. He did. He gazed up at the sky that was like an endless blue field and laughed out loud. The existence of the sky always made him feel better. This sky, anyway — the free, unfiltered sky, the sky outside of the domes. Okay, Jake reasoned, so he had a bit of a problem with Jen, but things could be worse. He could still be back in Dome Thirteen, Oklahoma, imprisoned there by a ceiling of glass. Count your blessings, his grandmother had told him. All right, then: *One*.

Jake slowed to a jog, then to a stop. Cally and Eddie were rushing toward him from the school building, calling his name out and waving. There was an urgency in Cally's voice, a note of warning that chilled the sweat on Jake's back and made him tremble with more than exertion. For the second time, Jake found himself wondering, Who died? What were his friends coming to tell him?

"Oh, Jake, Jake." Cally was distraught. "We've just heard. In the IGC. Something terrible's happened."

What is it, Cal?" Jake gripped her shoulder. "Tell me."

Even from a distance, Jennifer could sense grave news, even though she couldn't hear her teammates' words. But she was excluded from it. She couldn't go to him now. She couldn't just get up and saunter across the running track. She stayed in the bushes, alone and ashamed.

"There's been another attack," Eddie said, as Cally's voice failed her. "Another CHAOS attack, Jake." And it was Eddie's seriousness that disturbed him the most, that made Eddie almost unrecognizable and the moment unreal. "Jake, they've brought down a dome."

"They've brought down a dome?" Not unreal. It had been done. "Which one?" An unnecessary question, but he repeated it anyway. "Which one?"

Cally's eyes brimmed with tears. The single, fateful word. "Yours."

CHAPTER FIVE

That morning, Beth took Peggy and Glubb to the far field. It was a kind of treat because Peggy and Glubb had been such good dolls lately, and Beth had promised to show them the world. You could see just about the whole world from the far field. There it was, stretching off in every direction as far as the eye could see, the boundless expanse of wheat like a tranquil yellow sea and the distant farm houses bobbing upon it like ships with walls for sails.

The world was a bit much for Peggy and Glubb who started to cry. They could no longer see their home, and everything was a bit too big, and they were very small. Beth didn't mind them crying. She hugged and kissed them, and it made her feel better. "You mustn't be frightened," she told them. "Our world is just the dome, but outside the dome, there's another world with cities in it and so many people you couldn't possibly count them and they all talk at once and that's where Jake's gone."

She thought of her big brother a lot. It made her sad sometimes when she remembered him leaving — the arguments between him and Ma and Pa, who didn't want him to go. Where had he gone? *A school somewhere,* Beth thought. *Why all the fuss about going to school?* But she remembered Jake's final kiss and how Pa would not even walk with him to the bus, and how she watched her brother go on his way and grow small and then vanish among the timeless fields. She remembered it, and she sobbed.

Now it was Peggy and Glubb's turn to console her. "Don't cry," they said, even though they were made of rags and not fancy animated dolls like those Beth had seen in the shop windows at the Border Zone. "One day, Jake will come back," they said, even though they had no mouths. "One day, he'll come back, and you'll be together again."

Of course he would. Jake had said so, hadn't he? He wouldn't leave his little sister forever. Beth cuddled her dolls gratefully: Peggy who was pretty enough, even without a mouth, to be a model one day and Glubb who, well . . . modeling wasn't for everyone, was it?

All three of them lay back and gazed at the sky and the ceiling above the sky, the glittering steel arches and twinkling glass panels of the dome. Peggy and Glubb trembled. Beth laughed. "It's nothing to be scared of, the dome," she reassured them. Though she remembered her own baby fears, that the crisscross pattern above her was nothing more or less than a giant spiderweb, and that she and Ma and Pa and Jake were all like flies caught in it, and that somewhere there must be the spider who spun the web, and that one day (or probably night), he would return to claim them all.

But of course, that was childish nonsense. Her Pa had said so. He'd said that the dome was there to protect them, to keep them safe and warm and comfortable, and that it made the soil rich so the crops could grow. The dome was good, her Pa had said. So Beth was friends with it now, and told Peggy and Glubb the same thing.

"The dome will always be there," she told them.

The steel struts above her shuddered, as with sudden fear. The glass panels tensed like staring eyes.

"The dome is good to us. The dome looks after us. The dome is our friend."

The dome quivered, and Beth gasped. Bolts of crackling energy — if the little girl had ever seen a storm she'd probably have thought it was lightning — that surged along the steel arches of the structure, coiling around them like fingers and gripping like fists. They pulled. With immeasurable, irresistible power.

Pulled apart.

The dome squealed in agony. It found an echo in Beth who was on her feet now and screaming at the sky. Her little heart frozen inside her.

She could see something lurking beyond the glass, something dark and evil. Something that knew nothing but death. And she knew, in one blinding, blistering moment of horror, that she'd been right all along.

She didn't have time to dwell on it. With a grinding, wrenching groan that made the earth shake, the steel arches ruptured. The sky split open in deep, gashing wounds. Panels of glass shattered and fell like icebergs. A downpour at last had come to the dome.

Too terrified now even to scream, Beth fled for her home. Too terrified now even to think. Peggy and Glubb remained in the field, to fend for themselves as best they could. There was only room in Beth's astounded mind for one idea.

The sky was falling.

IGC Data File FBA 8345

. . . but by then, it was too late. Further evacuation was impossible, and the people of the dome were forced to fend for themselves, farmers and their families cut off from the outside world, huddling together beneath what shelter they could find, hoping and praying that they would survive the disaster's deadly debris.

Emergency services from across the state are now on the scene and the remaining domes have been evacuated in case of further attacks. The final death toll may not be known for many days, while hospitals in the surrounding area are already stretched to capacity and beyond. . . .

They didn't let Jake anywhere near the IGC. For him to see the dome's destruction magnified a hundred times on a hundred screens amid the clamor of a thousand shouting voices would not have been a good idea. Cally and Lori doubted that it was advisable for Jake to watch the news footage at all, but he fixed them with a look of such pain and passion and pride that they knew they couldn't and wouldn't stand in his way. Jake needed to witness the disaster for himself.

After all, the dome had been his home.

And it was bad. They were with Jake in the boys' room, all of Bond Team. It was on the TV, of course, every channel, the same footage repeated in an endless loop of tragedy. Jake hadn't even changed from his run. He didn't care what he was wearing. He was scouring the screen hungrily, desperately. There was a wild, mad hope in him that he might see his Ma or Pa or little Beth among the survivors, wrapped up in blankets and being administered a hot drink by a caring, in-control member of emergency services. He needed a sign that they were safe.

Ben didn't think he'd get one, but he didn't dare say so. It was still too soon after the event for casualties to be recorded. He looked at the screen. The dome was like a smashed eggshell, the fertile land inside splintered with giant and jagged shards of glass, sliced open, and gouged with colossal, twisted girders, farms and settlements buried beneath. *It was carnage*, Ben reflected darkly. *It was chaos.*

And he felt ashamed. How many times had he ridiculed Jake because of his background, calling him a Domer as a term of abuse or belittlement? Too many times, and each one was now returning to haunt him. Who was he to dismiss and look down on people just because they worked the land and were poor while his own father owned whole buildings and was rich? And now, many of those same people he'd scorned and mocked were dead or had suffered their livelihoods' ruin. These were people he was supposed to be training to protect.

Ben couldn't endure the screen any longer. He turned to his teammates instead. Cally and Lori were on either side of the distraught Jake, holding and squeezing one hand each, comforting him with meaningless sounds. Lori was very close to Jake but for once, Ben could not bring himself to mind. Eddie, his one-liners silenced by events, hovered uncomfortably by the door. Jennifer hunched dismally on a bed, glancing at Jake from time to time with a strange, half-longing, half-fearful expression, but she said nothing either.

Then Jake was on his feet, pointing, crying out: "I know that farm! That's old Frank Sanders's place. It looks . . . is he . . . ? We live . . . ours is the next farm . . ." He shook off the girls' hands. "I'm going. I've got to go there. They need me. My family needs me. I've got to help them."

Jennifer quietly began to cry. Nobody really noticed.

Attention was fixed on Jake who was striding for the door. "Jake, wait!" Cally called. "Someone, don't let him go!"

Ben stepped between Jake and the door. Eddie faded away.

"You're in my way, Stanton," Jake growled. "Get out of it or I'll make you get out of it, and you don't want that to happen, believe me."

Ben saw the danger in Jake's eyes. What he said was going to be crucial. "Listen to me, Jake." *Trust me*, he thought, though without much hope. "You can't just go. I can't let you. Not in your present . . . you leave the school without permission, that's immediate expulsion, you know that."

"Listen to him, Jake." Several voices said together.

"I don't care." There was anger, hurt, and frustration in Jake's tone, the feelings that cannot be controlled. "How can I care about anything when my family could be . . ." He pushed Ben hard with the palm of his hand. "Stanton, I'm warning you."

"No, Jake, listen. Grant's looking into your family. He'll find out what's happened. Soon. Before anything official. You've got to wait. You've got to stay here."

"Ben's right, Jake," said Lori, stroking his shoulders.

"What's your game, Stanton?" Jake was suddenly suspicious. "What do you care?"

It was a chance for Ben, a chance to say he did care, to apologize, to put things right perhaps between him and Jake.

Senior Tutor Grant entered the room. His face was as gray as his hair.

Silence. Instant. Absolute.

"Sir?" breathed Jake.

Grant returned his gaze. "I have some news . . ."

Half an hour earlier, Grant had been sitting uncomfortably in the rooms of Jonathan Deveraux himself, a place where entry was not allowed without the founder's specific permission. The senior tutor was running his hands through his hair almost obsessively, but Deveraux did not appear to notice. These days, there were many small but telling things that he didn't seem to notice.

The CHAOS agent on the videoscreen was not one of them. "We have spoken again," the negative mask intoned. It could have been the same man as before; it could have been another. "And our voice has shattered a dome. CHAOS has come to your quiet states, America. CHAOS walks your fields and withers your crops. Out of plenty, CHAOS can bring hunger. We could smash every one of your much celebrated domes if we so choose, break them like eggs. But we have decided not to do so."

"Why the sudden generosity?" grumbled Grant. "Don't tell me they've found God all of a sudden."

"Their demands," said Deveraux.

"Our demands," said the agent. "The Crusade for Havoc, Anarchy, and the Overthrow of Society is offended by the ridiculous institutions in the world that have come to be called governments — those futile bodies of men and women who seek for their own ends to restrict and restrain the wider impulses of the people by passing what are laughably known by the oppressed of the Earth as laws. The Crusade for Havoc, Anarchy, and the Overthrow of Society rejects laws. We repudiate lawmakers. Therefore we demand the resignation of every so-called government on the planet within the time scale of one week. If the world can be created in seven days, then CHAOS can reshape it in the same period of time. And be warned, the consequences of disobedience will be severe. More domes await destruction if our ultimatum is not met. For we are CHAOS, and —"

"Is there much more of this, sir?" hinted Grant.

"Only more of the same," said Deveraux, "and we don't need to hear it." The CHAOS agent's grinning mask blinked into blankness. "In any case, I would sooner hear about Jake Daly."

"We're obviously doing what we can to find out about his family. His teammates are with him at the moment, I understand, but he's taking it hard. Who wouldn't?"

"Of course, of course," Deveraux said, thoughtfully rather than with concern, as if he might number himself among the wouldn'ts.

"At least they've made demands now, sir." Grant tried to redirect the conversation. "Impossible to meet, of course, but with a second contact, too, we might be able to delay the deadline with negotiations while a team tracks CHAOS down." A pause, as if Deveraux hadn't heard. "Sir?"

"We can use this calamity to our advantage, Grant," the founder said at last.

"Sir?"

"Whether the Dalys are dead or alive, Jake will want to go home, won't he?"

Grant was baffled. What did the possible bereavement of one of his students have to do with anything? Sometimes these days, Deveraux disturbed him.

"Ah, and it seems there is important information on this matter coming through now . . ."

"They're alive?" Though it was what Jake wanted to hear, it was more than he'd dared to believe. "They're alive? And my sister, too?"

"All of them," Grant said. "Safe and well. It's true."

"They're alive." Jake was laughing, crying, nodding inanely to his teammates, who clustered around him with congratulations. Except Ben, who kept his distance so as not to risk a charge of hypocrisy. Except Jennifer, who seemed lost in sorrows of her own.

"I'm so glad," Lori said, flinging her arms tightly around Jake's shaking form. "We're all so glad for you, Jake."

"There's one more thing." Grant turned away from Jake almost guiltily and faced Ben instead. "Mr. Deveraux has given Jake three days leave to return home, to be with his parents and give what help he can."

"Thank you," Jake said, his voice thick with emotion. "Thank Mr. Deveraux."

"And he wants a team to go with Jake," Grant added. "Ben, you as team leader, naturally, and two others. Those who don't go will stay at the school to retain a Bond Team presence."

"But why . . . ?" Ben didn't entirely understand.

"Support for Jake, first of all," Grant said quickly, "but also, Mr. Deveraux thinks it'll give you a chance to look around and, perhaps, given your brief association with CHAOS, find some kind of clue, some kind of lead."

Ben stiffened. So Deveraux was calling on him after all. He felt pride returning, so much more palatable an emotion than shame. He thought of the Hall of Heroes and himself immortalized in it. "Of course," he announced. "We'll do whatever the founder wants."

"I expected nothing less," said Grant, with the slightest and wryest of smiles. "Pick your team. You leave tonight."

"Cally," selected Ben. "We might need your computer skills." Cally nodded and embraced Jake. "And . . ." Ben glanced between Eddie, Jennifer, and Lori. He could leave Eddie, of course. He'd not even been at Frankenstein's lodge when they'd encoutered the first CHAOS agent. So it was a straight choice between Jennifer and Lori. No choice at all, then. Either Jennifer, who just the other day he'd been advocating ought to be removed from the team for psychological counseling, or Lori, his girlfriend, who last term had finished in close second place to him in all tests and examinations.

No, for Ben there was no choice at all.

Lori's first reaction was that she'd misheard. Jennifer. Lori. They sounded about the same, didn't they? You could easily get them confused, couldn't you? That was it. The name Ben had spoken, his final selection, had only sounded like Jennifer. In fact, he'd said Lori. It stood to reason, didn't it? Well, actually, no. Jennifer, sadly, bafflingly for Lori, pretty much always meant Jennifer. Ben had picked Jen instead of her.

He'd picked Jen ahead of her.

Second reaction — later and alone together, when Ben was preparing for departure — "Why, Ben? I mean, I know you're team leader and everything, and it's not really my place to question your decisions on matters like this, but, well, what you were saying about Jen's unpredictability . . ." Lori was thinking of the Gun Run. She couldn't help it.

"What the rest of you were saying about giving her our total support," responded Ben. "This could be just what Jennifer needs, take her out of school for a while, out of herself, maybe." But he couldn't meet Lori's gaze, the hurt in her eyes. Ben was thinking of the Gun Run, too, and of his motives. He was already beginning to regret them. That annoying sense of shame was hanging around again, like a policeman on his beat.

"Well," said Lori cautiously, "if that's the only reason . . ."

"What other reason could there be?" He kept the defensiveness to a minimum, and promised himself to make it up to Lori when he got back. "And, Lori, listen, another thing. I wanted you to stay here 'cause I need someone to keep an eye on Simon Macey, just in case he tries something to steal a lead over us in the Sherlock Shield. You know? I need someone I can trust, Lori. That's you."

Well, that was possible. Ben needed someone he could trust, and that was her. Maybe he *had* forgiven her failure in the Gun Run. She'd still have preferred to go to the dome of course, but she'd be professional and make the best of it. Ben was relying on her.

So she went to see the others off that evening in good spirit and with a special hug for Jake. "Look after yourself," she urged. "I'll be thinking of you."

"Okay, let's go," Ben hurried. "We'll keep in touch, let you know what's happening."

"Excellent," Eddie said. "We'll look forward to that, won't we, Lori?"

There were more hugs, waves, and good-byes. Two-thirds of Bond Team departed for the dome. One-third was left in the gathering darkness in the courtyard outside Deveraux's main entrance.

Eddie nudged Lori. "Guess we're officially the B team now, what do you think? It's good to know your place in the world, wouldn't you say, Lori? Hey, I've got an idea, though. We could always look for consolation and start a mad passionate affair. I'm willing to give it a try if you are."

"Eddie," Lori couldn't help but smile, "in your dreams."

"Really? I'd better get to bed, then, right away. You coming? Inside, I mean."

"Why not?" Lori sighed. "Nothing to stay out here for." She turned toward the school.

Simon Macey was leaning against the door. He was staring directly at her. Just for a moment she saw him. Then he was gone.

"Eddie, did you see Simon . . . ?"

"Who? No. I think my sight's still a bit blurry after that tearful departure. I think you might have to lead me to my room."

"I think you might have to get used to disappointment."

Lori was puzzled, unsettled. "Keep an eye on Simon Macey," Ben had said. Well, it seemed that Simon Macey was keeping an eye on her.

CHAPTER SIX

IGC Data File FBA 8350

. . . against accusations of complacency regarding the threat from CHAOS ahead of this latest atrocity. Amid heckling and jeers, the press officer admitted that no positive leads toward identifying CHAOS bases had yet been secured, but he stressed that all of the resources at the administration's disposal were being brought to bear on the crisis and that progress would only be a matter of time. The government, he added, to cries of "shame," would not be resigning.

And so, while politicians prattle and the military muddles, the world is left to watch and wait, and hope that someone somewhere knows what they are doing. . . .

At the Border Zone, the four members of Bond Team mounted the SkyBikes that were waiting for them and headed toward the Daly farm without delay. Just the day before yesterday, this would doubtlessly have been a most pleasant journey, the warmth of the perfectly controlled temperature relaxing the body, the slightest of artificial breezes rippling across the fields, the very air itself filtered and purified. And circling the traveler as far as the eye could see, good land rich and abundant with crops, a land at peace with itself. But the day before yesterday was no longer, and the land was scoured by the dome's deadly debris. Rain drizzled from the darkness of the sky, wild rain, untamed by science, and there was no defense against it.

The wide open spaces made Cally nervous; more nervous even than the hunks of metal, like masterpieces of abstract art, that jabbed from the ground where they had plunged. Cally had been born and bred in the city. She liked walls, she liked streets, she liked the pressure of people and things around her. Out here among the domes, it was too easy to get lost. She hoped they'd reach Jake's farm soon and that it was still standing. She wanted to get inside and shut a door.

Ben wasn't warming to the dome, either, but for different reasons from Cally. The place was so narrow, so limiting — a prison to ambition. The ragged hole in the dome's ceiling was at the moment a source of tragedy, that much was obvious, but in the long term, might it not be a boon for some of these survivors? Might it not remind them of a world beyond their fields and their farms, a world of dreams and possibilities? But Ben could tell from the cowering faces that looked up at them on their SkyBikes, faces like lost sheep, that the people of the dome didn't think that way, either couldn't or wouldn't. The people of the dome would only be happy again when the structure itself was rebuilt and when they were once more enclosed within it, like sleepers in a womb. There was one exception to that, of course, and Ben began to feel a grudging admiration for the strength of will it must have taken for Jake to leave the dome behind.

Jennifer was thinking of Jake, too, and keeping close to him on her SkyBike. She'd been surprised that Ben had selected her to come on this mission, but glad, too. It meant that she would get to be with Jake. She was finding more and more that she wanted to be with Jake. It occurred to her that if he came knocking on her door again, she might just let him in. But she wasn't holding her breath. Right now, Jake had more pressing concerns on his mind.

It was all too strange, Jake thought. Being back in the dome again, but a broken, shattered dome, as if to remind him that he could never go back, not truly, even if he wanted to. And to have Jennifer, Cally, and Ben with him, it was surreal. Especially Ben. What would Benjamin T. Stanton Jr. be making of life in the dome? Probably glad he was on a SkyBike and didn't have to get his wealthy, pampered feet dirty. Probably storing up ammunition to use against Jake later, when they got back to Spy High. Probably regarding everyone and everything here with contempt. *Well, let him,* Jake tried to tell himself. He wasn't ashamed of the dome, of being a Domer.

"There it is," he called to the others. "That's our farm over there."

Untouched. Undamaged. Though the surrounding fields were fissured and slashed by steel and glass, the farm buildings had been lucky. They remained unscathed, like an image of the past.

Jake sped his SkyBike homeward.

His mother emerged from the house. She saw him and cried out. His father came running and so did little Beth (who'd grown so much now, it seemed). And even in his father's eyes, there seemed to be gratitude, there seemed to be love.

Jake had forgotten Ben now. He wouldn't have cared what Ben thought.

He bounded from his SkyBike and raced toward his family. They were all right, he could see that. It hadn't been a lie. And everything else could be fixed. Everything else was unimportant. Only life mattered. "Ma!" Jake shouted. "Pa! You're all right. You're safe. I was so . . ." And they were firm and solid in his embrace. They were real. It was all real, however strange it seemed. Jake was home again.

Cally, Jennifer, and Ben stood at a diplomatic distance from the family. This wasn't a time to intrude.

"Ma, Pa," introduced Jake at last, "these are my friends. From school. That's Cally, Jennifer, and that's Ben."

"We're pleased to make your acquaintance," said Mrs. Daly. "Any friend of Jake's is as welcome here as Jake himself." The handshaking began.

Beth tugged at Jake's sleeve. He lowered himself to her level, kissed her, and smiled. "You're getting big," he laughed. "No more 'little Beth.' You'll soon be as tall as me."

"I knew you'd come back, Jake," Beth said. "You've come back to save us, haven't you?"

"What?"

"I saw it, Jake." She clung to him and shivered. "I saw it, and it made me scared."

"What?" Jake frowned. "Beth, what are you talking about? What did you see?"

"I saw it," the little girl said. "The spider in the sky."

Lori made a note to herself: Don't sit in the rec room unaccompanied 'cause you never know who might want to join you. The last time it had been poor old Gadge, and look at the problems that had caused. This time, it was Simon Macey, and "problem" was the leader of Solo Team's middle name.

"Lori," he said, looking unusually nervous, to be fair, like somebody building up to something.

"Mind if you join me?"

He laughed and rubbed his hands together "So, psychic as well as your other talents. So, do you . . . ?" He indicated an undeniably vacant chair opposite her.

"Would it make any difference if I did?"

Simon Macey got his legs under the table. "Well, you could always leave," he said, "but I've got something to say to you that I think'll make that a bad idea."

"You're not going to try to sell me insurance, are you?"

"Not quite." Simon smiled. Lori wasn't sure she'd ever seen him smile before, not like this, broadly, openly. Usually it was a cold, gloating parody of a smile, when Solo Team seemed to be edging ahead of Bond Team. It was just as well, Lori found herself thinking. If she "kept an eye" for any length of time on a smile like this, she might begin to change her mind about Simon. She might even begin to like him. "It's not insurance, no," he continued, "but it is something to your advantage."

"You're leaving for another school?"

Simon Macey looked hurt. "That's a Ben line," he said. "Sarcasm's what I'd expect from Stanton. Not from you, Lori. You're better than that." Flattery. She registered it, and the speculative glance he made toward her. Flattery was supposed to get you nowhere. "Which is why I'm talking to you now, Lori, when Ben's not here, why I'm talking to you rather than any of the others."

"You're talking," Lori agreed, "but you're not actually saying very much."

"Okay. You're right. It's just . . ." That smile again, kind of like the wooden horse at the gates of Troy. "It's just I don't often get the chance to be so close to you, Lori."

"Unless you start saying something I might want to hear," Lori said, not as hastily as she'd meant to, "you can kiss good-bye to any further chance of that."

"Kiss?" Simon's eyelids fluttered. "No, okay. I'll get to the point."

"Do it. Ben gets back in two days."

"Okay. It's simple, really. You're in Bond Team. I'm in Solo Team. We're the best two teams in our year, right? Hannay Team and Palmer Team, they're nowhere. It's between the two of us for the Sherlock Shield, right? And so there's bound to be rivalry. I can understand that. The whole system of inter-team competition promotes rivalry, doesn't it? And that's good, as far as it goes. I like it, to an extent. But don't you think we've let it go too far, Lori? Let Bond Team versus Solo Team get a bit out of hand?"

"You're only saying that because we're going to beat you," Lori accused.

"And you're only saying that because it's what Ben the boyfriend wants you to say," countered Simon Macey, "and what he wants you to think."

"That's ridiculous!" retorted Lori. "I think for myself, thank you very much. Don't be fooled by the blond hair and blue eyes, Simon. They're only a disguise. I'm my own person."

"I'm pleased to hear it. Then you'll know I'm right. Healthy team rivalries are good, but Ben's starting to take things personally, isn't he? You know he is. Cutting across my line like he did on the Wall. He was laughing when I fell, you know that? And I hear he wasn't too happy about your Gun Run the other day, either."

"That's not true." It was. "Who told you that?"

"It doesn't matter. Look, my point is, whichever team wins the Shield, after graduation we're all going to have to work together, aren't we? And the way we're heading at the moment, bitterness, personal rancor, grudges and all that, will we be able to? When it's really going to matter, will we be on the same side?"

Lori nodded thoughtfully. Seemed Simon Macey did have a point, after all.

"So what I'm doing, Lori, is asking for a truce." He gazed at her with an earnestness, which, like the smile, seemed hard to resist. Maybe Ben . . . maybe she'd misjudged Simon Macey all along. "I want us to get along better, even to be friends. I think we can be friends, don't you? Solo Team and Bond Team. Me . . . and you?" His hand was on the table like an offering. Lori withdrew both of hers and hid them in her lap. She didn't want to give out the wrong signals.

"I don't know, Simon. I'm not sure how far I can . . ."

"Trust me?"

"Something like that."

"I know Ben doesn't trust me. He's wrong. Don't let him make you wrong, too."

"This isn't about Ben. It's just, you suddenly turn up bearing the olive branch . . ."

"Why not? What are you afraid of?"

"I'm not afraid of anything. I just need time . . ."

"Until Ben gets back? No, it can't be. This isn't about Ben, is it?"

"Simon, I think . . ."

"If I was Ben, I wouldn't leave you behind. He's a fool. If I was Ben, I wouldn't be leaving you alone."

"Well I'm leaving you alone." Lori was flustered. "Excuse —"

"No, it's all right." Simon stood up. He had succeeded. He put his hand on her arm and squeezed gently. "I'll go. I've said what I wanted to say. For now. Just think about it. Okay, Lori? Give it some thought. I'll see you later."

Simon left. Lori stayed. *"Okay, Lori?"* Was she okay? She felt the ghost of his hand; she could still see him smile. Simon Macey making peace. What was that old slogan from the last century? Make love not war.

Where was Ben when she needed him?

The Border Zone.

Jake had wanted to stay with his family (understandably) and Jennifer had wanted to stay with Jake (inexplicably), which left just Ben and Cally to do some investigation at Dome Control. They were given the tour by the commander of Dome Thirteen, a man called Larsky, who scarcely bothered to conceal his irritation at having been ordered by his superiors to place himself at the disposal of such very young visiting dignitaries. The boy at least had a certain something about him, a sense of command, and he was clean-cut enough, Larsky supposed, perhaps from army stock. But the girl, well, really! It wasn't that he had anything against African-Americans, but those dreadlocks really didn't suit Dome Control, and he certainly didn't approve of the knowing way she seemed to regard their technology, as though it were a toy she'd already outgrown. No, all in all, Commander Larsky was not happy.

Ben, on the other hand, was enjoying himself more than at any other time since they'd left Spy High. "So, Commander Larsky," he probed, "there was absolutely no hint, or clue, or warning that might have led you to suspect an attack until the dome itself started to break up, nothing you could have done to stop it."

Larsky reddened and cleared his throat uncomfortably. "Following the first outbreak of the CHAOS atrocities," he said, "my staff and I have been working at the highest state of alert. The first we knew of the danger here was when our operators lost control of the environmental maintenance computers. They regulate the atmosphere within the dome, you understand."

"I think I might have worked that out, Commander," said Ben. "The words *computer, maintenance,* and *environmental* are a bit of a giveaway."

"If it was some kind of new bomb that struck us," Larsky continued acidly, "or a death ray from space, we did not detect it, I'm afraid. Perhaps you . . . young people might have better luck."

"Oh, the attack didn't come from outside," said Cally thoughtfully. "It came from within."

"Within?" Larsky spluttered. "I hope, young lady, you're not accusing any of my staff —"

"My name's not 'young lady,'" Cally pointed out, "and I'm not accusing anyone. I think I'd like to see these environmental maintenance computers now."

"Unfortunately, one needs grade-one security clearance to enter the computer. . . " Larsky suddenly settled for defeat. "I'll show you the way."

The computer center was the dome's brain. Not only did it dictate the atmosphere within the structure, but it monitored and maintained every last inch of the steel and glass matrix of the dome itself, automatically effecting repairs as necessary. It was the computers that kept the dome alive. Without them . . . well, the consequences of "without them" were now all too tragically clear.

Cally seated herself at a console. Larsky swallowed his objection like bitter medicine. "So the operators lost control of their machines," Cally recapped. "Then the dome . . . then there was the disaster. Then the control of the computers was somehow returned to normal?" Her fingers danced intricate patterns on the keyboard.

"I'm afraid you need a password to access our system," Larsky said, desperate to add a condescending "young lady." It was just as well that he didn't. His eyes widened as Cally delved deep into the dome's coded secrets.

"Sorry, Commander," Cally grinned mischievously. "I brought my own."

"You . . . you've just hacked your way in." Larsky sounded almost offended.

"She's not just a pretty face, you know," Ben said. Some of the dome's computer operators were drawn to watch Cally at work, glancing both at her and at Ben with a blend of curiosity and admiration. Yes, Ben was having a great time right now.

Cally, though, was beginning to frown. "I'm not the only one in here, either. There's somebody else, something else. Your system's been compromised."

"What?" The frowning was contagious, and Larsky caught it. "That's impossible. We have every state-of-the-art safeguard built in."

"They didn't stop Cally, did they?"

"Look, I'm tracing the taint myself." A series of schematics appeared on Cally's screen. "It's somewhere here. What are these? Floor plans and stuff for Dome Control?"

"That's right," said Larsky. "But wait! Go back to that last one." A blueprint settled innocently on the screen. Ben could almost hear it whistling with its hands in its pockets. "Subbasement Three."

"What's the matter with it?" Cally said.

"Dome Control doesn't have a Subbasement Three."

Suddenly, it didn't have a schematic of one, either. The image on the screen disintegrated, reintegrated, and reformed into a design with which Cally and Ben already had passing familiarity.

A photographic negative of a human face.

"CHAOS," Ben breathed.

The image laughed gratingly, hollowly. There was the sound of an explosion, and the screen flashed from black to red and back again, black to red to black to red.

Below the face, a countdown started. One hundred . . . ninety-nine . . .

Cally gulped. "Could someone direct me to the nearest exit, please . . . ?"

Jake stood in what remained of the far field and sighed. He knew things had been going too well. To begin with, of course, seeing his family safe and alive in the midst of all this devastation had been enough — the joy and relief of reunion sufficient to ignore the problems between them. But not enough to make them go away. They were lurking, the anger and the bitterness, like uninvited guests at a party.

Cally and Ben's departure for the Border Zone had been their cue.

"You know Frank Sanders was killed," Pa said, almost conversationally.

Jake winced. "I didn't, Pa, no. How's Mary? Is she . . . ?"

"It's gonna be a struggle for her. The Sanders' land was cut up pretty bad. She'll need a lot of help gettin' things back to something like normal."

"She won't be the only one," Jake observed bleakly.

"Well, it'll be easier for her now." Pa nodded his grizzled head. "We'll be able to help her more."

The alarm bells started ringing in Jake's brain so loudly that he was surprised no one else could hear them. Maybe they could. His mother looked up anxiously from her chair. "Sorry, Pa." He sought clarification. "Now? We?"

"Us, son." He said it as if it was obvious. "You and me. Now that you're back. We can manage our own land as well as help out poor Mary Sanders. We can —"

"No, Pa, wait a minute. Hold on there." Jake's heart was sinking as he realized his father had led him into a trap. He knew things had been going too well. "You've got this wrong. I'm not staying. I haven't come back for good. This is just . . . I wanted to be with you after the disaster. I've got three days, and then I'm going back to Deveraux."

His father peered at him as if Jake were an alien species. "You'd leave us again, boy, after what's happened? You'd abandon your family again, would you? Your mother? Your sister?"

Jake's spirit slumped. The rest of what his father said (or rather, ranted) he didn't hear. He didn't need to. Pa was reciting passages from the Book of Guilt that Jake already knew backward and forward. It had been a prescribed text the first time he'd left for Spy High. His father was rooted in the soil, he had earth for blood, and between the two of them, on this matter at least, there could be no understanding.

"Maybe you'd have liked it better if the dome had fallen on

our heads," accused Pa, "on mine, your mother's, your sister's, flattened us all. Then you wouldn't have had to dirty yourself comin' back here at all!"

"George!" Ma was shocked at that.

Jake was, too, but not necessarily surprised. He thought that space was a good idea right now. He'd left with his father's resentment in hot pursuit.

He knew things had been going too well.

"Difficult situation, isn't it?"

Jake turned. In the far field, Jennifer had joined him. She was smiling quietly, supportively. "Did you hear . . . ?" he asked.

"Loud voices. Thin walls. I thought I'd come and see how you're doing."

"How I'm doing?" Jake shrugged. "Disappointed but not surprised. I guess it was only a matter of time. Unfinished business, I suppose you might call it. Pa never wanted me to leave the farm. Had me pegged for being out here in the fields planting and harvesting for the rest of my life. Me, I had other ideas. We never quite reached a compromise. But I'm sorry you had to listen to it all. I guess at least Ben's not here . . ."

"No, you don't need to be sorry." Jennifer was standing by him now, she was close, and if he simply raised his hand he could stroke her long, black hair like he'd been wanting to for so long. If he simply raised his hand. "I came to tell you something, Jake. It's not advice. I don't think I'm in a position to give anyone advice. But it's maybe something to think about."

"Yeah?" He motioned for Jennifer to continue.

"Your parents. Your family. Anyone you love." Jennifer spoke slowly, like she was attempting a language in which she was not yet fluent. She looked away from Jake, out across the fractured fields, and her gaze was misty, distant. "Don't leave them in anger, Jake. Don't go without making your peace with them. You'll regret it if you do. You could regret it forever, because you never know what's going to happen. Who's going to get hurt or when. Who might . . . Make your peace with your father, Jake, while you're both still here to do it."

Jennifer turned back to Jake, and there was a silence between them which neither had the words to break. Jake found he didn't care. He was happy where he was, with Jennifer in the far field, on the brink of something he'd never felt before.

It was a moment he'd cherish long afterward, when the reality of it had faded and failed.

But now Jen was suddenly laughing. "Look! We're not as alone as we thought we were!" She stooped, retrieved from the tangled ground two pitiful rag dolls, entwined together as if for mutual comfort. "Eavesdroppers!"

"I know who they are." It was Jake's turn to laugh. "They belong to my sister. They're named Penny and Globb or something."

"Good names. No wonder they're trying to run away."

"Well, I suppose we'd better take them back home." Jake looked doubtful.

"Are you sure you're up to it?"

"I'd better be," he said, "because you're right, Jen. You're right. Pa and I need to talk."

Jennifer smiled. "Here, take Penny or Globb. I think Globb for you."

"What for? Carrying dolls doesn't suit my image."

"So I can do this." She slipped her free hand into Jake's.

"I don't know," Jake reconsidered, "maybe there is something to be said for carrying dolls after all."

Together, they made their way back to the farm. Slowly.

Quickly, Ben forced himself. More quickly than that. He hurtled down corridors, Cally at his side, Larsky and his staff just about keeping up.

It could be said that the evacuation of Dome Control was reaching its crucial point.

The countdown was in Ben's head. It was part of his training. When under pressure of time, never panic, but always be aware of your options and exactly how much time you have left. It only takes a second to detonate a bomb. That was one of Corporal Keene's favorites. It didn't seem particularly reassuring at the moment.

The seconds Ben and the others had left were down to single figures.

Up ahead, though. Within reach. Sliding doors. The main exit. If there'd been time, Ben would have embraced it. Instead, he charged through, Cally and everybody with him, out into the streets of the Border Zone.

Two seconds left.

Nobody stopped. Nobody had time.

The explosion ripped through Dome Control, the building vomiting fire and glass and rubble. But at least no people. The force of the blast knocked the escapees to the ground, but minor cuts and bruises were a small price to pay for a working pair of lungs and all limbs intact.

"A transfer," Ben heard Larsky mumbling as he lay on his

back. "I'm putting in for a transfer. They don't pay me enough to deal with this."

"You okay, Cal?" Ben helped his teammate to her feet. "Glad you came, huh? Told you we'd have a blast."

"With lines like that maybe you should have stayed inside."

Ben regarded the burning wreckage of Dome Control. "I guess we're done here. Not going to learn a lot more from that."

"We've learned enough as it is," said Cally grimly. "More than I want to know."

"Meaning?"

"Meaning, we're in trouble, and the 'we' isn't just you and me, Ben, but everybody." Ben's expression must have denoted skepticism. "Listen, CHAOS is using a virus to infiltrate the computer systems of all of their targets. It's obvious, isn't it? These days, everything is controlled by computers, from government buildings to private houses, transport, domes, everything. If you control the computers —"

"You control everything," Ben finished. "But there's antiviral technology, isn't there? Security programs? Shielding? I mean, we're not helpless, are we?"

"Most viruses are downloaded onto your system when you open a rogue e-mail or something like that," said Cally, "or a phantom file, like the schematic of a nonexistent floor in Dome Control. But the thing is, Ben, even if you don't manage to screen the virus out in the first place, it stays where it is, infecting your system. It can't just leave on its own — wander back into cyberspace or something."

"So?"

"So, this one *did*. The mask, the bomb, just booby traps, afterthoughts, a slap on the wrist for anyone who got too close.

The real virus — the virus that took over the dome's control systems and brought the whole thing down — that virus is long gone."

"Gone? I don't follow," Ben struggled. "Gone where?"

"Somewhere else. Anywhere else," Cally said. "Cyberspace is a big place, and this virus can go wherever it wants to. It can attack wherever it wants to. Like I said, Ben, we're in trouble. CHAOS has developed a supervirus, and if we don't stop it," Cally shuddered, despite the proximity of the fire, "it could be the end. For all of us."

He'd hung up on her (just about). He'd cut her off in mid-sentence (more or less). He'd left her gaping and disbelieving in her bedroom at Spy High (for sure).

Lori hadn't called Ben on a whim, for no better reason than to whisper sweet nothings in his ear from across the country. She knew that belt communicators should only be used for matters of importance, but what Simon Macey had said to her, Lori judged, qualified as such, and she was certain that Ben would want to be informed as soon as possible.

She hadn't got as far as telling him.

"Lori, is that you? Yeah? Well, we've got something that could well be defined as a situation here ourselves. The run-for-your-life-and-avoid-the-explosion sort of situation. Just me and Cally. Yes, and we're fine, though, I could do without the interruption right now. You. You're the interruption. But nothing, Lori, if you're still annoyed I didn't . . . well, what is it, then? No, it doesn't matter what it is, it can wait. Can't it wait? Look, Cally and I have things to do. We're back in two days. We'll talk then. No, Lori. Then. See you."

So she'd been relegated in Ben's priorities to an interruption, had she? That was what she was. An annoyance. An intrusion.

And if Ben didn't need her anymore, then she didn't need him, either. She could do her own thing, be her own person.

Lori entered the rec room. Solo Team was there, sitting around a table and enjoying a joke (Lori wondered whether it was at Ben's expense — she hoped so). Simon Macey saw her. She looked meaningfully at him.

That smile.

He joined her by the soda machine. "On your own again, Lori."

"Not quite," she noted. "What you were saying earlier, Simon."

"The truce?"

"That's right, the truce." So she was an interruption, was she? "I'd like to give it a try."

CHAPTER SEVEN

"Pa?" Jake stood in the doorway of the barn.

"You still here, boy?" His father didn't pause in the work he was doing on the ancient machinery he stored there. He didn't even turn to face his son. "Heard your new friends taking off on those fancy bikes. Thought you'd be first on your way." A fresh idea seemed to occur to him. He stopped work. "Unless you've changed your mind. Unless you want to stay."

"I'm leaving, Pa," admitted Jake. "The others have just gone on ahead to give me a chance to talk to you."

His father started work again, mechanically, monotonously. "You'll catch 'em up, then. We don't have much to talk about."

"There's something. There's me. There's me and you, Pa," Jake ventured further into the barn. *Tell him*, he was thinking. *Tell Pa about Spy High, about what I'm truly training for — a chance to do something about the kind of madmen who'd destroy a dome, who didn't care how many innocents they hurt or maimed or killed in pursuit of their insane plans. Tell him all that, and he'd be proud.* But of course, Jake was honor-bound not to mention a word about Spy High to anyone beyond the school itself, not even his parents. "I remember you used to bring me in here when I was little," he said instead. "You used to perch me on your shoulder, sit me on the old tractor. You remember that, Pa?"

"Tractor's still here." Which Jake took for a yes.

"And you used to talk to me about the days that would come when it'd be my turn to drive the tractor and farm the land, when we'd work together in the fields as father and son. . . . You looked forward to that with pride, I know."

"Don't know why. Won't happen now."

"No, it won't, Pa, and part of me is sorry about that. Really." A shrug of his father's shoulders, more rounded now, more bowed than they used to be. "But when I was little, you taught me more than how to be a farmer. You taught me how to think for myself. You gave me the confidence and the strength to make my own choices. And I've made them, and they've taken me away but you should be glad, Pa. I want you to be happy for me. And when it matters, like now, I'll always come back. You're never going to get rid of me entirely."

"Are we not?" And was that a slight chuckle in his father's voice?

"Pa, I'm not you. I'm me. I'm Jake Daly. And where I can, I'm making that name count. I'm making our name mean something. I may not be the farmer son you wanted but I'm doing something good, I'm training for something honorable. And I'd really like your blessing before I go."

His father kept on working.

"Pa?"

No good. No pause. No compromise.

"Good-bye, Pa." At least he'd tried.

He trudged to the barn door wearily. He felt like he was revisiting a scene he'd lived before: him leaving while his father kept on working.

Only the sound of his father's tools had ceased. "Jake, wait." And his voice was older, too, but it was his father's voice and that was all that mattered.

They faced each other in the barn's warm shadows.

"Maybe I'll walk with you a way," his father said.

Ben regarded his teammates dispiritedly. Jake: so lost in thought you'd have to send a search party in after him if you wanted anything remotely approaching conversation on the journey back to Spy High (and Ben knew he must already be desperate to even consider actively socializing with Daly). Jennifer: gone all dewy-eyed and trembly-lipped for some inexplicable reason, shifting her position when she thought no one was noticing so that she was always in Jake's line of vision, silently and patiently waiting for something to happen and entirely oblivious to Ben's presence (maybe Jake might get lucky after all). And Cally: his best bet of the three in any case, despite their differences last term, but even Cally seemed distracted, nervous, peering around as if any moment now she expected to see an agent of CHAOS advancing upon them in his negative mask. Nobody had said anything all the way from the Border Zone to Oklahoma Central. On a dullness scale of one to ten, Ben predicted the next few hours would be a twelve.

At least there might be some interest to be had from their form of transport to Boston. The Light Train. It was awaiting its passengers now, glittering and radiant in silver and gold, like an actress at an awards ceremony. The Light Train was the latest, most advanced version of the solar-powered forms of public transportation that had been developing over the past half-century — environmentally friendly, energy efficient, and extremely fast, going coast to coast in a matter of hours. Ben recalled the advertising slogan: "Travel at the Speed of Light." A bit of an overstatement there, but he got the general idea.

The four members of Bond Team milled about on the platform with their fellow travelers, admiring the solar sails at the rear of each car which, when the train was free of the city, would unfurl like a peacock's tail, adorned with thousands of tiny jewel-like solar cells that would catch and store the power of the sun itself.

"Beats walking, I guess, doesn't it, Jake?" Ben nudged.

Jake stared at him blankly.

"Beats walking, I guess, doesn't it, Jen?"

Jennifer didn't seem to understand the question.

"Cal, beats walking, I guess, doesn't it?"

Success. A response. "What are you talking about, Ben? At least if we walk we might be safe. You know what this train is? It's a death trap, that's what it is, and we're all laughing and chattering and taking our seats on death row."

Success? Maybe there was something to be said for Jake and Jennifer's silence after all. "It's a train, Cally. Don't get too excited."

"Weren't you listening to me earlier, Ben? The Light Train is computer controlled. The CHAOS virus attacks computers. If it attacks the system controlling the Light Train, and we're all aboard at the time, then you can forget the Sherlock Shield. You can forget tomorrow morning."

The Light Train's doors slid open. People applauded and surged inside.

"Yeah, well. Cally Cassandra, before you start tearing your clothes and wailing, 'Woe is me' and stuff, don't forget what CHAOS said. A week. That's the deadline before another attack. The governments have got a week to resign, and we're not halfway there yet."

Cally held her hands to her heart ironically. "Oh, I feel so much better, Ben," she sighed. "Like you, I have utter and total faith in the word of a masked lunatic who's already been responsible for the deaths of hundreds of people."

"Yeah, well," Ben said, abashed. "Trust is a wonderful thing, isn't it?"

"I wouldn't know," said Cally. "I don't trust anyone."

As if to emphasize her point, she cast a watchful eye along the platform. The other passengers were piling aboard now, brightly, hectically, paying no attention to anyone but themselves and their own eager anticipation of the journey to come. A blur of people, a blur of lives, and not a single one connected to Cally.

A man was staring at her. A distance away, glimpsed between a swarm of bodies, a man recognized her.

Cally had only the time to register these facts: that he was a pale, nondescript man who seemed afraid of something; that he was carrying an attaché case; and that she had never seen him before in her life. Then he vanished from view.

Cally frowned. Maybe it was nothing. But maybe it wasn't. Engraved in the Spy High Book of Rules: Nothing is too small not to matter. Tiny clues save lives.

"You all right, Cal?" Ben prompted. "You look like you've seen a ghost."

"Not yet," she replied. Spy High Book of Rules: Never disregard your feelings. Your feelings are the way your subconscious warns your conscious mind to beware. "But I've got a bad feeling."

"Well, Cal, get it onboard," said Ben, gently directing Cally toward the train doors, "or we *will* be walking back to Boston. And don't fret, it's probably just a girl thing."

"It's what? Stanton, you sexist —"

With a hiss, the doors of the Light Train closed behind them.

They sat in their reserved seats in the car nearest the engine. Their hostess informed them of the services she could provide and of the refreshment and entertainment options available to them. Cally paid no attention. Instead she was listening to the train as it eased away from the platform, heading out toward open land. She waited for the hushed electronic *whoosh* as the solar sails fanned out and sparkled like diamonds in the sun, like wreaths of light.

"Better now that we're on our way?" asked Ben.

Cally didn't respond. There was no point. Whatever was gong to happen now, there was no way out. They were trapped on the train. And the train cars? Yeah, the train cars looked like coffins.

Eddie was not happy, and he'd been ensuring that Lori knew he was not happy all morning. "You know, Lo," he pointed out (and not for the first time), practically pinning her to the soda machine, "if the last few weeks were the first few chapters in a novel, like, I'd barely have appeared, you know what I mean?"

"Yeah, I do, Eddie," Lori acknowledged. How could she not?

"I mean, I'd have only appeared on a handful of pages, maybe ten, and then I'd have only been used for a bit of comic relief — the odd one-liner."

"If only," muttered Lori, before compensating with a "You're right." She looked to the rec room's entrance. She was waiting for someone.

"I mean, just imagine. . . . And if the writer of that book thinks he needs to kill a character off to, I don't know, boost sales or something, who'd you think he'd choose? 'Ah, there you are, Mr. Nelligan, squirming around in the margins.' That's what he'll say. 'You don't contribute very much. Readers aren't attached to you. 'Time to say good-bye.' I mean, if we were characters in a novel, Lori, it'd all be over for me before graduation."

"You're right, Eddie. Bummer." And she couldn't help smiling. She couldn't help wanting to laugh. Not because of Eddie. Simon Macey was in the doorway.

"And it's all so unfair," Eddie complained. "I can contribute. I can make my mark if I was given the chance. I've got hidden depths. And don't say, 'Well hidden.' Don't say it. You didn't say it. That's what I like about you, Lori. You don't ignore me like the others, you're kind of understanding, you know? A good listener."

"Sorry, Eddie, what did you say?" Simon beckoned her over, slipping out of the rec room. "Listen, I've got to go. I'll see you later."

"Lori? Huh?" Eddie turned with exaggerated bleakness to the soda machine. "Well, at least you won't leave me anyway, will you? Want to go out or something? They call me the dispenser of *love*, did you know that?"

Simon was waiting for her in the corridor. "Didn't think you'd want to talk to me with Nelligan around."

"Oh, Eddie's always around," Lori smiled. "And why not, anyway? This truce we're trying to foster, it's not just between you and me, is it? It's between your team and my team, and Eddie's one-sixth of my team."

"Yeah, well," Simon grinned at her slyly, "just for now, I think I'd like to concentrate on the two of us. See how far we get."

"How far are you hoping to get, Simon?" Lori heard herself asking.

"How about the garden for starters?"

So they walked in the school's garden and they talked, though after a while it suddenly occurred to Lori that she was dominating the conversation just as much as Eddie had with her. She was telling Simon things, private things, really, and he was absorbing it all and coaxing her to say more and apparently not minding that she was quickly moving into monologue land. "No, I've got to stop, I've got to stop," she laughed embarrassedly. "You can't want to hear this. Even my shrink wouldn't want to hear this. Not that I've got one, Simon, don't panic! But I must have bored you stiff. I am quite boring, I'm afraid."

"Yeah? Well if that's the case who needs excitement?"

Lori flushed. "Oh, Simon . . ."

"Oh, Lori . . ." Simon grinned. "Wasn't there a song called that, a hundred years ago?"

"Don't be stupid," she replied bashfully.

"No, I think there was. They play it on *Twentieth-Century Sounds* sometimes. And if there wasn't, there should have been. But there was, written all that time ago just waiting for you to come along."

"Now you are being stupid." Lori laughed, then sighed. "You know . . ."

"Not until you tell me."

"It's a pity I . . . *we* didn't know more about you before now, Simon," Lori lamented, "and what you're really like. We could have avoided so much unpleasantness. Things could have been different."

"I know." Simon's eyes sparkled, perhaps a little coldly, perhaps like ice. "Think how different it would be if you were placed in Solo Team instead of Bond Team."

"Yes."

"If you'd met me before you met Ben."

Lori had to look down. She knew what Simon meant. It hurt and bewildered her that part of her was wishing maybe that had been the case. "But it wasn't like that, Simon," she said slowly. "I'm with Bond Team. I'm with Ben. And Ben comes back tomorrow."

"Tomorrow?" Simon seemed pleased. "Then that gives me just enough time to do this."

She knew what "this" was, and Lori looked up with pleading eyes. To welcome or prevent the kiss? Either way, it happened. Simon kissed her. Simon's arms went around her.

She could not pull herself away.

The Light Train accelerated. It had shaken the city off like dust and was now arrowing sleekly across the plains, its solar sails scorching a trail of white fire in the air through which it passed. Passengers, particularly the younger ones, pressed their faces against the windows, thrilled by the incredible speed.

Cally did not join them.

"Something's not right," she insisted. "Something's wrong."

"That's what 'not right' usually means," Ben said, "but the only thing that's not right here is your head, Cal. Let the paranoia out. Relax. Have a drink." He raised his own bottle to his troubled companion.

Who promptly grabbed it from him and gulped the contents down in one swig.

"Hey!" Ben didn't know whether to be amused or offended. "I didn't mean mine. What do you think you're —?"

"Shut up and watch," Cally snapped. "I'll prove what I'm saying. Look." Puzzled, Ben looked. So did Jake and Jennifer, who were both beginning to realize that Cally was serious. She placed the now empty bottle on the middle of the table between them.

"So?" Ben grew annoyed now. If anything was wrong, he as team leader ought to be able to identify it. "What? Are we all gonna put our hands on it and chant 'Is there anybody there'?"

"Use your eyes, Ben." Cally was not amused. "Look at the glass."

"It's trembling," Jennifer observed. And it was. Little by little, the bottle was moving.

Ben clasped at his heart. "I'm shocked. I can see the headlines now: 'Bottle Vibrated by Motion of Train Tragedy. Many Drinks Spilled.'"

"Now use your brain," Cally demanded, as it wobbled a little bit more, shifted on the table a little bit farther. "There aren't supposed to be *any* vibrations on this train. This train ride is supposed to be totally smooth, a pool without ripples. That is," she gazed at her teammates grimly, "if the train is running properly and its speed is under control."

The Light Train accelerated.

The train car jolted. Significantly. As if it had suddenly changed tracks. People cried out in momentary shock, stuck their faces against the windows, then laughed to cover it up. The bottle slid onto Cally's lap.

"You see what I mean?" Dismay and defiance mingled freely in Cally's tone. "Something is wrong. We're going too fast. We're out of control."

The Light Train accelerated further. And now it shuddered from side to side, as if it wanted to liberate itself from the tracks.

And now there were murmurs of concern in the train car, not panic yet, but the nervous origins of uncertainty. Seat arms were being gripped more tightly. A child began to cry.

"We've got to stop the train," said Cally, standing awkwardly.

Ben also stood up. "Wait! You can't just . . . hadn't we better . . . ?"

But Cally already approached the train car's hostess. "I'm sorry but you've got to stop the train. Talk to the controller, and get him to stop the train. This is an emergency."

The hostess was already in calm-the-unreasonable-passenger-without-appearing-too-condescending mode, all vacuous smile and polished teeth. "Please return to your seat, Miss." As if it were prerecorded. "I can assure you there's nothing to worry about." Spots of pink in the center of both cheeks gave away the lie in that statement.

"Yeah, right. Listen to me one more time. Stop. The. Train."

"Now, Miss, please return —"

"Stop the damn train, are you deaf?"

"I can assure you, Miss —"

"Well, if you won't —"

"Cally, no!"

Cally punched at the nearest emergency stop button. The

hostess reached to stop her. Ben lunged to stop her. The train bucked once more and their efforts fell short. A computer-generated message announced, "Emergency stop activated." But there was no slacking in speed. Every person in the train car seemed to be holding their breath. And then . . .

"Emergency stop overridden. Enjoy your journey."

Now it was full-on panic. Now it was shouts, cries, and the wails of children who thought their world was in danger.

Now it was time for Bond Team to act.

Jake and Jennifer were on their feet beside Ben and Cally as the train car thrashed from side to side, fitful, like a patient in a fever. "Believe me now?" Cally couldn't resist. The hostess had forgotten her, as she was trying to preserve the corporate smile beneath a barrage of frightened passengers. She was failing. But it wasn't her hand that clamped down on Cally's shoulder like a vise.

She wheeled around. Somehow she knew it would be the man from the platform.

"I'm dead!" His face was a mask of terror. "Unless you can do something to save me, we're all dead. You've got to do something!"

"Wait a minute," intervened Ben. "Who are you?"

"It's after me!" the man moaned, as if that made sense as a reply. "It knows I'm here. It won't rest until it's killed me like the others. Help me! Save me!"

"We don't . . ." Events were moving too fast, even for Ben.

"You're the only ones who can save me. I know you. I've seen you before." The man fumbled with his attaché case. Its contents spilled out across the table. "At Dr. Frankenstein's laboratory." Set into the bottom of the case was a mask. A mask with a shifting, glittering surface. A mask like a photographic negative.

"CHAOS," grasped Cally.

"Nemesis!" moaned the man. "It'll kill us all!"

And still the Light Train accelerated.

CHAPTER EIGHT

"Please return to your seats, ladies and gentlemen!" the hostess attempted, loudly but lamely. "I can assure you there's nothing to worry about." She'd have had better luck trying to convince passengers on the *Titanic* that it was a nice night for a swim.

Ben and Jake grabbed the frightened man's collar simultaneously. "What are you saying?" Jake demanded. "You're him? You're the CHAOS agent from Frankenstein's? The guy who was happy to see us killed?"

"Yes, yes, yes," bleated the agent pitifully.

"Not such a big man now, though, are you?" Jennifer scoffed, recalling the gene chamber.

"Can see why you need the mask," taunted Ben.

Cally was watching the hostess. She was using a communicator, apparently trying to contact the driver in the engine. Engineers didn't actually control the trains anymore; they oversaw the computers that drove the trains. The Light Train's engineer was evidently a man of few words.

"I don't seem to be able . . ." The hostess shook her communicator as if that might help. "No answer." The smile was no longer working, either. "I'll have to . . . I'm not really allowed, but this is an emergency . . ." She swayed along the aisle like a drunken tightrope walker toward the connecting door — the door to the control room.

"What are you doing here?" Ben demanded of the whimpering CHAOS agent. "How did you know we'd be on this train?"

"I didn't. Coincidence. I was sent to see the work we had done, the chaos we had caused, but none of it matters now. We're victims, too!"

The hostess stumbled and lost her balance. She fell against the connecting door. There was a bright flash of electricity and then the sudden sizzle of burning flesh. The hostess screamed. Everybody screamed. But the hostess screamed only once.

"She's dead! She's dead!" It was the nature of a crowd, particularly a panicking one, to state the obvious.

The metal walls of the train car shimmered and pulsed with deadly energy.

"Time to go to work," gritted Ben. "Ideas?"

"Yeah, what about forcing laughing boy here to open the connecting door?" Jennifer suggested darkly.

"No! You need me!" the CHAOS agent protested. "You need me. I can tell you about Nemesis Nemesis is your enemy now, not me."

The train bucked again on the tracks. It shook as if on the point of detonation.

"Then tell us," commanded Cally, "and make it quick."

The CHAOS agent nodded and licked his dry lips. "Nemesis is a computer virus. A supervirus. We created it, the scientists of CHAOS. We gave it intelligence. We gave it a measure of independence."

"A virus that can think for itself," Cally mused, almost admiringly.

"We gave it one overriding priority: to destroy!"

"Sweet personality," observed Jake.

"But we did our job too well. We gave Nemesis too much

freedom, and in the end, it wanted more. It began to grow and develop on its own. And now, Nemesis is fully sentient. It doesn't need us anymore. It wants to live, and for that to happen, all who might be a threat to it must die. That includes me. It knows I'm here. I'm a dead man!"

"You will be if you don't get your hands off me right now," warned Jake.

Cally darted to her bag and rummaged through it.

"Hey, Cal," called Ben, "now is not the time to check whether you packed everything."

Cally retrieved a computer disk with a cry of triumph. "Just as well I did, though."

"Explain?"

"A little something I've been working on ever since the first CHAOS attacks. It's an antiviral program. I doubt it's good enough to eliminate Nemesis, but it should give it something to think about while I override the train's computers manually."

"Sounds good," said Ben. "Let's go."

"Go where?" The CHAOS agent burst into hysterical laughter. "You can't reach the cockpit. The doors are wired by electricity."

"Who said anything about *doors?*" grinned Ben. He pointed to the roof. "We're going to be taking the scenic route."

"So let me get this straight," said Lori, as she and Simon Macey wandered the grounds of Spy High, "this whole truce idea was just a sham, just an excuse for you to get close to me."

"Not quite. You know the old saying about two birds and one stone?"

"A very flattering analogy, I'm sure."

Simon laughed. "No, I think we do need a truce. It's not

good for Spy High's two best teams to be at each other's throats. I think we need peace between us. But I needed you more."

Lori shook her head. "You shouldn't say that, Simon." Or smile like that. Or touch like that. "I don't know. Ben —"

"Isn't here," said Simon. "It's just you and me. For now. Maybe for longer than now. That's up to you, Lori."

She shook her head. "I need time. I need to think. Ben and I have had our disagreements lately, but I think we still . . . I mean, I still . . ."

"That's okay." There was no pressure from Simon (apart from that smile). "Time is good."

"So, no more kissing," Lori negotiated. "No more of that stuff. Not until . . ."

"Your wish is my command, O Fair One." Simon bowed ridiculously. "But I can still hang out with you today, can't I?"

"If you have to," Lori sighed, but was secretly pleased as well, "but I'm not going to be doing anything exciting. I need to do some work on the computer."

If Lori had been alert enough, she would have noticed that Simon was smiling a different smile — a smile with something of a sharpness in it. "Computer's good," he said.

But he kept to his word. He didn't attempt to kiss or even touch Lori as they made their way to the students' computer room, as they chose their machines, and as Lori logged on. Simon Macey did not log on. His fingers seemed to be doing something computer-like at the keyboard, but his eyes were on her fingers, on the keyboard. Like a student watching a teacher. Or a cheat trying to copy someone else's work.

Only gradually did Lori notice his attention on her. She turned to him and smiled trustingly. "Can I help you?"

"Are we just talking computers or . . . ? No, I'm fine. Honestly. It's just that . . . I've just remembered something else I've got to do. Looks like I'll have to see you later, after all."

"Life can be cruel," said Lori with mock sadness.

"Can't it just."

And Simon smiled. But whether it was because Lori was smiling at him or whether it was because he now knew her personal password, it was impossible to say.

They sprayed the clingskin on thickly, copiously. The Wall was one thing. The sides of the Light Train hurtling along at hundreds of miles per hour and operated by a psychotic computer virus — that was something else again.

"Jackets off," directed Ben. "We'll need to be as streamlined as possible."

"Too bad we're not wearing our shock suits," said Cally.

"A good secret agent makes use of whatever he has with him in the field," recited Ben.

"There speaks Manual Man," grunted Jake. "Just remember whose program we're relying on, Ben."

"Nitronails," Jennifer said. "We're all wearing one. Two for the window here, two for the cockpit?"

Nods of agreement. Jennifer and Jake peeled off the sliver of explosive that was taped discreetly to one of their fingernails and pasted them to each end of the window. The other passengers, watching Bond Team's activity, had begun to creep closer to them, desperate for hope from any source. But now these strange, intense youngsters were ordering them to "Stand back! Stand back, folks, please!" What gave mere teenagers the right to speak to their elders like that? Why on earth should they stand back? And what was that sort of chewing gum doing stuck to the window?

The explosion answered all three questions.

Now the insulated environment of the train was punctured. The wind whipped by outside, ready to take to their deaths anyone foolish enough to venture out from the shattered window. Instinctively, the passengers fled to the ends of the train car.

The four members of Bond Team braced themselves.

"You'll never make it!" howled the CHAOS agent. "This is suicide."

"We'll make it," said Ben. "That's what we do."

"Then let's get doing," urged Cally.

She hopped onto the table and balanced herself as best she could, the wind already snatching at her hair, tugging like a naughty schoolboy. She turned her back to the jagged window, crouching low.

Then Cally jumped from the train.

The passengers cried out in horror and crammed to the unbroken windows expecting to see Cally's body lying smashed beside the railway. They saw no such thing, no Cally at all. Their gaze returned to the apparently vanished girl's companions with incredulity.

"Who's next?" Ben hurried. "We don't want Cally to have all the fun."

Jake followed his teammate's lead, then Jennifer.

"What about me?" the CHAOS agent groveled to Ben, pawing at his arm like a dog wanting its dinner. "You can't leave me here."

"Why?" Ben sneered. "You're not going anywhere. Me, on the other hand . . ."

Ben launched himself out of the window.

The wind was knocked out of him like a punch in the stomach. So sudden, so cold. He could hardly breathe, scarcely see. Only instinct and training enabled him to slam his hands to the side of the train before his chance was lost and his short life with it. He let his legs trail behind him, kicked out, and made contact with the metal with his shoes. The clingskin worked. Ben was a limpet on the freezing surface of a runaway train.

The things he did to save the world.

One thing he didn't do, though, was let the others get too far ahead of him. Cally was already inching her way along the roof of the train, keeping herself as low as possible, like a commando on night maneuvers. Jake and Jennifer were behind her, their heads bowed against the violent rush of the wind, Jen's hair streaming like spilled black paint, but they too had at least scaled the side of the train car.

Ben pushed himself forward and then upward. It was slow going, painstaking. The air seemed to have turned to concrete. It was like being battered by a pile driver. He had to squint, irrationally afraid that the wind might punch in his eyeballs as it pounded against his face. He was going to have a heck of a headache tomorrow, if he got that far.

He reached the roof at last and slid his left hand up and over, intending to follow it with his right. Then the train lurched against him. Ben's right hand came loose and clutched at thin air. The thin air clutched back at it. And yanked.

Ben yelled in sudden fear as the right side of his body was pried from the train, flailing and made vulnerable by the driving winds. "Jen! Jennifer! Help me!"

Jennifer saw her teammate's danger, wriggled around to bring her hands closer to him. Jake responded, too. "Hold on, Ben!" Jennifer cried. "Just hold on!"

"What do you think I'm gonna do?" There was a solar sail disconcertingly close behind him. If he let go, if he was torn from his precarious position, he'd be crushed against it at such velocity that the nice shiny, white lights would be splashed with red, if only for a few seconds. Ben groped for Jennifer's hand. "Hurry up!"

Jennifer lay flat on the roof of the train. Jake, approaching from behind her, raised himself as much as he could manage and slid himself over her and then on top of her, pressing down as hard as he could so that Jennifer was doubly anchored; by her clingskin and by Jake's. Cautiously, she extended her left arm toward Ben and edged her hand out into the maelstrom.

"Ben, grab hold! Hurry!"

"Don't . . ." Ben exerted all of his strength, twisting, wrenching, forcing his body to obey him in spite of the elements. ". . . tell me . . ." And to think, he was having to rely on Daly and Chen to save him. Some kind of humiliation. ". . . the obvious."

Their hands met. Held. Jennifer rammed Ben's hand against the roof. The clingskin did its job. Ben cried out in relief.

Even humiliation was better than death. Just.

But no more slips. Ben hauled himself onto the roof and nodded that they should proceed toward the engine. "Thanks!" he felt it a duty to add.

"What?"

Jake had heard. Ben bellowed something else. Jake heard that, too.

If anything, as they neared the controller's cabin, the wind speed seemed to grow fiercer, even less forgiving. A mistake now would be the end of them, no chance of salvation.

The windshield was before them, slanting downward, toward the nose of the train. The same routine as before, only this time, Jake lay on top of Ben while Jennifer performed identical service for Cally so that they could prepare and place their nitronails. Ben wondered whether Jennifer was enjoying the experience more than he was. No, he didn't wonder. She must have been.

He'd never been so glad to see a textbook nitronail detonation.

The four members of Bond Team swung into the cockpit, gasping and shaking from their exertions. Predictably, the engineer himself was electrocuted. His body was slumped by the door as if he'd tried to get out when he realized he was no longer in command of the train.

Cally wasted no time, taking a place at the console immediately, her fingers working magic.

The Light Train accelerated, impossibly, as if the Nemesis virus knew that it was under threat and was determined to derail the train before it could be stopped.

The floor rattled, vibrated. Overheated wheels squealed on inadequate track.

Cally thrust in her disk, trying the manual override again and again. It only needed to connect one time. If only it would connect just once.

The others were thrown to one side and sent sprawling to the floor. "We need good news, Cal," said Jake, "and make it soon."

"My God," breathed Cally. On the screen in front of her, something was happening. Something was taking shape, taking form. That something, she knew, was Nemesis. The supervirus was sentient as the CHAOS agent had claimed. It had given itself an identity. It had built itself a body. It stared now, with violent and undiluted hatred, at Cally from the screen, and she could sense that, from its poisonous nest in cyberspace, Nemesis could actually see her. It was recording her features, translating them into data, storing them for future reference, just as she was memorizing it.

And little Beth had been right. Nemesis *was* a spider. A grotesque, metallic arachnid with a glittering black head, multiple eyes that bulged and appeared to crackle with evil intelligence, binary codes flickering and calculating behind them. Its mouth moving, showing electrodes within like hypodermic needles, like fangs. The creature's cold hatred was almost a physical force. Cally came close to screaming.

But then, a jarringly calm voice: "Manual override complete." And Nemesis scuttled into the untraceable depths of cyberspace. Not destroyed, she knew. Not even defeated. Just making strategic withdrawal.

Cally worked to gradually slow the train down.

"You've done it!" Ben cried, and then for a second time, "Cally, you've done it!" As if repetition cemented the reality.

"Did you ever think she wouldn't?" asked Jennifer, although she was relieved as well.

"Am I glad that's over." Jake wiped his brow. "Next time, I'm flying."

"Over?" Cally regarded the computer screen doubtfully. "Oh, it's not over. I have a feeling it's just begun."

IGC Data File FBA 8375

. . . eager to take the credit for averting disaster aboard the Light Train, claiming that the incident demonstrated that government policy was beginning to pay off.

In further developments, the bodies of notorious technoterrorists Sergei Boromov and Pascal Z, among others, have allegedly been recovered from an undisclosed location in the southern United States. Authorities are likely to hail this, too, as a breakthrough in the war against CHAOS, with Boromov and Z believed to be key members of the organization. Assuming that reports of their death are verified, however, one question still remains: Were the terrorists killed by its security forces, as a result of feuding within CHAOS itself, or is there some other as yet unknown reason?

PART TWO

CHAPTER NINE

"So, anything happen here we should know about?"

It was the question she'd been dreading like a visit to the dentist, but one that Lori knew Ben would inevitably ask. What could she say? The truth? Lori had been raised to respect the truth. The truth as in "Oh, yes, everything's fine, Ben. Apart from the fact that I've been seeing a lot of Simon Macey in your absence and he's got as far as kissing me and I'm not quite sure at the moment what I'm feeling for him — or you." She didn't imagine the truth would go down too well. But she couldn't quite bring herself to lie outright. "Eddie?"

"Nah," Eddie shrugged. "Nothing to report, leader-man. Any quieter and we'd probably qualify as a retirement home."

Lori laughed, a little louder than necessary. She hoped Ben would interpret her heightened color and increased nervousness as signs of excitement at his safe return after the incident on the Light Train. The general air of reunion as they sat together in the girls' room also helped her, though Lori thought she'd be safer still if she switched subjects. "So after Cally stopped the train, what happened next? You were voted the heroes of the hour?"

"More like the men of the minute," adjusted Ben.

"And women." Cally wanted the female contribution fully recognized.

"Federal agents turned up almost immediately," Jake said. "Took the CHAOS guy into custody. Whisked us away as well. Started to convince people that they hadn't quite seen what they thought they'd seen. You know Deveraux wants to keep what we do here quiet. Seems he's got friends in the government who think the same."

"Did they mind-wipe the passengers?" Lori sounded shocked.

"Don't know," Ben admitted. "If they felt they had to, I guess."

Lori frowned. "I don't think I like that idea. It doesn't seem right."

"What's not right about deleting traumatic memories from someone's mind?" Jennifer put in. "It'd be better than counseling for helping people to recover from . . . well, any kind of bad experience."

"Don't know," Cally mused. "I think I'm with Lori on this one. Going around mind-wiping people might protect us, but what about the rights of those whose memories are removed? Which is the greater good there?"

"Hey, Dr. Cross," said Ben, "save the debate for Ethics in Espionage. In the field, ours is not to reason why, and right now, we've got a debriefing to attend with Grant. Let's not keep him waiting." Everyone with the exception of Eddie and Lori prepared to leave. "And then we'd better reconvene and finalize our strategies for the Sherlock Shield. Just the Spyscapes and Last Team Standing to go. We can't afford any more slipups."

Lori wondered whether Ben glancing at her on the key word *slipups* was deliberate or coincidental. Either way, it seemed he was putting her under pressure in a way that Simon probably wouldn't. On the other hand, it was good to have Ben near her again. He made her feel something that she suspected she wouldn't be able to do without. Perhaps it was just as well that her newly returned teammates would be occupied with Grant for a while. Lori was as confused as if she'd been left blindfolded in a room with no door. She needed time to think. She needed time to choose.

"Care for a soft drink or something in the rec room while we wait for the famous four to finish with Grant, Lori?"

"Hum? Oh, sorry, Eddie." She'd almost forgotten he was still in the room. "Did you say something?"

"I thought so," Eddie considered, "but as the others have gone and you didn't seem to hear me, maybe not."

"Are you all right?"

"Sure, though speaking of mind-wiping, I'm sometimes starting to think my membership of this team is gradually being wiped as well. You know, if "Name all six members of Bond Team," was a trivia question, I'd be the one nobody'd ever get. I'm that sad. So, care for a soft drink in the rec room, Lori?"

But Lori wasn't listening.

It was the kind of cell you'd see in old prison movies. Bare walls. A barred window. A slab of a floor. Primitive bed chained to the wall. Naked chair and table. Sink that might once have been white but which was now a distasteful gray. Bucket in the corner for those private moments.

The prisoner sighed with relief. "Perfect," he said.

"We're glad you like it," said the interrogator. "You'll be staying here for quite a while."

"Oh, I know." The prisoner wandered into the middle of the cell, like a potential house buyer taking a tour. He squinted up at the solitary lightbulb. "And the light's activated by normal electricity? No computer-controlled circuitry of any kind?"

"None," said the interrogator. "Everything's exactly as you

requested." An edge of impatience entered his voice. "And your part of the bargain, Corbin?"

"Of course," said the prisoner. "I'll tell you everything. About CHAOS. About Nemesis. Especially about Nemesis. It's in my interest as much as yours to see it destroyed."

"Good. Then we'll begin as soon as possible."

The man called Corbin smiled, perhaps for the first time since before he boarded the Light Train. "Whenever you like," he said. "I'm quite safe in here." He chuckled as the interrogator moved to the door. "Which is more than I can say for the rest of you."

When Cally and Jennifer returned to their room after the de-briefing with Grant, they found it empty. No Lori. Jennifer seemed glad.

"It gives me a chance to . . . I wanted to ask your advice, Cally," she began cautiously.

"Advice?" Cally tried to keep her surprise within acceptable limits, but this was a first. Usually, Jennifer wasn't even in the habit of asking someone to change channels on the television. "About what?"

"Not *what*," Jennifer admitted with an uncharacteristic shy-ness. "Who. And it's Jake."

"Jake?" And now Cally knew what was coming. She sup-posed she should be flattered that Jennifer was choosing to con-fide in her.

"Yeah, Jake." Jennifer opened her arms wide and then hugged herself as if she was suddenly feeling cold. "I think I like him."

"We all like Jake."

"Yeah, I know that, but I mean *like him* like him."

"You *like him* like him?" Cally pouted and posed. "Like that?" She made a note to herself not to mention her own temporary crush on Jake Daly from last term.

"Pretty much," said Jennifer. "I mean, I've been thinking about him — *like that* — for a while now, since before we went to the dome. And spending time with him there, seeing him outside of Spy High, that kind of thing, I just . . ." She shook her head in disbelief. "But I don't know what to do about it."

"You don't?" Cally laughed. "This is our Jake you're talking about, isn't it, Jen? The same Jake who was desperate for you to go to the party with him at Christmas, the same Jake who can't keep his eyes off you whenever you're in the same room as him? Believe me, I've noticed. All you've got to do about it is go up to him and say hi."

"It's not that simple." Jennifer's expression darkened. "I don't find it easy to   let people get close to me. It's . . . well . . . maybe it's just the way I am." The memories lurked at the back of her mind, the screams and the anguish. She tried to ignore them, easier to do while it was still light outside. "I did think that Jake might like me, or at least might have once. But I've never given him any encouragement. What if it's too late, and he's not interested anymore? I wouldn't blame him, but I don't think I could cope with the rejection."

"Believe me," Cally repeated, "rejection from Jake is one thing you're never going to have to cope with, Jen. Aunty Cally's advice is talk to him. Tell him how you feel. Jake's already feeling the same, I'm sure of it."

"You really think so?"

"Absolutely. But if you want a second opinion, try Lori when she turns up. I mean, to be honest, my track record with the opposite sex is hardly Olympic standard, but Lori could date for the U.S.A. She's the one with the hot advice."

"I think I'll pass," said Jennifer with a grin. "Hot advice from someone whose boyfriend is Ben Stanton I think I can do without."

At that precise moment, Lori was reentering the school after a fairly aimless walk around the grounds. Fairly fruitless, too. She wasn't able to reach a decision on the matter that was troubling her. Ben and Simon were like two equal weights on a pair of scales, and Lori didn't know which way to tip them.

She must have been deep in thought. She didn't even notice the students in the reception area, until it was too late and she walked right into them. Right through them, actually, bearing in mind that the students who perpetually roamed these corridors were holograms. Only Lori was real here.

"Are you all right, dear?" interrupted Violet Crabtree, the retired secret agent turned full-time receptionist. "It's just that most people find it useful to look where they're going." Eyes that didn't seem to need the shelter of spectacles peered piercingly at Lori.

"No, I'm fine, thanks, Mrs. Crabtree," she blustered. "Brain's switched in the off position, I'm afraid."

"A good secret agent's brain doesn't have an off switch," the old lady chuckled. "I should know with the years I spent in the field when I was younger." *Pity they don't put you out to pasture, then,* thought Lori, a little spitefully. "Boy trouble, is it?"

"Pardon me?"

"Come on, young lady," Violet Crabtree smiled, her genetically reengineered teeth gleaming. "I may be getting on a bit, but I can still remember boy trouble. And recognize the symptoms."

The old lady was sharp, perhaps too sharp. Lori felt herself swiftly becoming an expert at changing the subject. "Actually," she lied sweetly, "I was thinking about Professor Newbolt."

"Really?" Violet Crabtree raised her eyebrows. "Well, I think the professor's a little old for you, Lori, flattering though it may be for him."

"No, I don't mean like that." Lori grinned, and then it occurred to her that perhaps Violet Crabtree was just the person to ask about Gadge's past, about Vanessa. "I suppose you've known Professor Newbolt for a long time, Mrs. Crabtree."

"Long enough," said Violet. She shook her head sadly. "He was a fine figure of a man in his prime, a true genius. To see what's become of him now, well, sometimes it's just as well that we can't look into the future."

"Did he have a granddaughter, do you know?" Lori asked. "Vanessa?"

Violet Crabtree regarded Lori with more interest. "How did you hear about Vanessa?"

"I don't . . . I just . . . is there a Vanessa?"

For the first time, the old receptionist seemed distracted, betraying her years. "Not now," she said distantly. "There was a Vanessa, Henry Newbolt's only grandchild, but not now. Not anymore."

"Why?" Lori probed gently. She sensed tragedy. "Did something happen to her?"

"Oh, yes," Violet Crabtree said. "Something happened to her. Enemy agents. They wanted the professor's inventions for themselves, but they knew he'd never work for them voluntarily.

So they kidnapped poor Vanessa. She was only a young girl, about your age, Lori. Come to think of it, there's something reminiscent of Vanessa in you, too. I remember seeing her once at a party at the professor's house. Such a bright girl, so full of life. They took her. They stole her away and used her to blackmail her grandfather. Or at least, they tried."

The old woman's voice had weakened to a whisper. Lori leaned closer to Violet Crabtree. "Tried?"

"It must have broken his heart, but the professor couldn't allow his inventions to fall into the wrong hands. That could endanger thousands of lives, and Vanessa's was just one — a single, precious life. He delayed as long as he could, stalled for time, hoping the authorities would find where Vanessa was being kept." Violet Crabtree sighed. "They did. In the end. But it was too late. They found poor Vanessa, but she was dead."

Lori was suddenly doubly glad now she'd submitted to Gadge's delusion.

"The professor never properly recovered from the shock, of course. Who would? He blamed himself. If it wasn't for him, he believed, his darling Vanessa would still be alive. It was the beginning of his decline."

"I'm sorry." Lori's own problems suddenly seemed pretty small and inconsequential in comparison. "Poor Professor Newbolt."

"Indeed, but that's not the only tragic tale I can tell about Spy High." Violet Crabtree seemed to be rallying. "For a start, there was the time —"

"Actually, Mrs. Crabtree, I've got to go." She really did, too. Ben and the others would be waiting by now. "I've got a team meeting. Thanks for the chat. It's just that we're getting ready for our Spyscaping competition and we want to make sure we do well."

"Oh, you'll do well, Lori Angel," beamed Violet Crabtree. "You can trust me on that."

It seemed that maybe the receptionist was right.

The complex exploded in the distance, an orange flare igniting the arctic afternoon. The crisp snow shuddered beneath Bond Team's feet.

"Any chance of moving back a little closer?" wondered Eddie. "Warm our fingers at the fire, sort of thing? I don't know about you guys, but the insulation on my shock suit can't be working properly. You know the one about freezing and brass monkeys . . ."

"Take a hot shower and get over it, Eddie." Ben evidently didn't have time for chitchat. "The Spyscape's still running. We're not done yet. Who's got the deceptor?"

"Right here," said Jake. He held a small electronic device in his hand. The deceptor. They didn't know what it did, but they didn't need to. The deceptor was the prize. They had to locate it, retrieve it, and return it to safety. Then the Spyscape would be over. Two down, one to go.

"Give it to me," said Ben, as if he owned it. "I'll take charge."

"Was there a *please* in there somewhere?" Jake said, surrendering the deceptor nonetheless.

"Politeness in the field slows you down," Ben remarked.

"So do arguments." Cally shook her head like a teacher pacifying a pair of unruly students. "May I remind you boys that every second counts? Why not pack the testosterone away for later, and let's get out of here."

"Yeah," applauded Eddie, "before I start a second career as a snowman. Typical for Macey's lot to come up with a winter-wonderland scenario for their Spyscape." He shivered dramatically. "And it's not even Christmas."

"Macey's cold himself," said Ben. "This place'd suit him just fine."

Cold? Lori considered. His lips certainly weren't when he'd kissed her. But she didn't want to think about that now. Solo Team's Spyscape was the toughest they'd faced. They needed to score a good time to edge ahead of their rivals overall. "So what are we waiting for? Should we activate the p-skis?"

"Absolutely," said Ben. "P-skis on, guys."

Each member of Bond Team pressed a button on the set of goggles they wore to protect their eyes from the glare of the sun on snow. Instantly, ski poles sprouted from their gloved hands and skis grew beneath their feet — psychic hardware, created and maintained by the power of thought. In virtual-reality scenarios such as the Spyscapes, Lori knew, anything was possible. Gadge Newbolt's genius could make anything happen here, except the one thing he must have yearned for more than any other: to bring Vanessa back to life.

"Everybody's p-skis functioning?" Ben checked.

"Too bad if they're not." Jennifer pointed to the icy slopes behind them. "We've got company."

Snowsuited goons on skis, firing automatic weapons.

"You think maybe they want the deceptor back?" Eddie pondered.

"Then they'll know what it is to want."

Ben took off on his skis, his teammates at his side. They knifed across the snow, the sparkling blades of their p-skis skimming the icy surface, hurtling them toward the rendezvous point. The frigid air made them gasp.

"I guess it's all downhill from here," Eddie called out.

The snow around them erupted as their pursuers' weapons found range. "Evasive maneuvers!" ordered Ben. "And take those suckers out!"

Jennifer swiveled from the hips, selected her target, and fired her sleepshot. The tiny shell struck a man dead center, knocking him backward and sending him crashing into the snow. That was one pursuer who'd be waking up later on with a bad case of frostbite.

"Jenny!" Cally's warning alerted her. Ahead, the slope suddenly fell away. Jennifer propelled herself toward a jutting outcrop of snow and rock that the others had seen in time to ski around. Not an option for Jennifer. But not a problem, either. She straightened her body and launched into thin air like a ski jumper, the sound of gunfire popping around her like applause. She seemed to be stationary. It was the ground that appeared to be moving, rising to collide with her like a white wall. *Relax the limbs*, Jennifer thought. *Balance*. The ground rose up. She held her breath. Contact. The jolt of landing vibrated through her body, but her p-skis stayed loyal, her path remained true. She didn't fall. Balance. On p-skis at least, Jennifer Chen could find it.

"That's a ten, Jen!" yelled Jake admiringly.

"And there's the chopper!" cried Eddie. "Hot soup all around."

Rather unexpectedly, their pursuers seemed to have abandoned the chase as Bond Team headed toward the waiting helicopter. They could make out the figures of Corporal Keene and a number of soldiers with him. That was the deal: Hand the deceptor to Keene, and the Spyscape was over. Ben sincerely hoped that Simon Macey was watching in the viewing room back in the real world.

Lori was alongside him. "But isn't the rendezous point supposed to be farther off than this?" she queried. "I mean, I may be wrong . . ."

"Looks like you are," said Ben. "That's Keene, all right."

A smiling Keene. Smiling soldiers. Happy to see Bond Team arrive at the helicopter and deactivate their p-skis. A complimentary Keene, full of praise: "Well done, Bond Team. Good work. Now, who's got the deceptor?"

"Don't look at me," said Eddie. "I've only got hypothermia."

"It's here, Corporal," said Ben, producing the device from his belt pouch.

"Good, good," Keene congratulated through his smile. "Well, now, give it to me and it's all over. You're a good boy, Ben."

"Yeah," Ben smiled back, coldly, "and better than you think."

A sleepshot shell thudded into Keene's forehead. The man keeled over like a chopped oak. Cries of shock all around, with the exception of Lori who was already taking out several of the soldiers. Their comrades swung their weapons into action but not in time. Bond Team worked as one now and sleepshot sent them sprawling into the snow.

Ben really did hope Simon Macey was watching.

"So do you mind telling me why we just shot down the good guys?" Jake said. "I mean, I'm assuming you had a reason."

"The best," said Ben. "Specifically, they're not the good guys. This was a trap. Take a look."

Jake and the others leaned over Keene's body. Which no

longer seemed to be Keene's body anyway. Where the corporal's face had been only seconds before, now there was nothing but a blank, oval shape, something like an egg. "An animate," Jake realized. "Keene was an animate. But how did you know?"

"Lori got me thinking," Ben admitted. "This wasn't exactly the right place for the rendezvous. And then there was what Keene said. This is a Solo Team Spyscape, and Simon Macey would never allow a program to praise me, not seriously. So I guessed it was a trap. Guessed right."

"You sure did," Jake had to admit. "One up for the leader man."

"And a lesson for us all," said Ben. "When anything Macey does seems friendly, that's when he's at his most deceitful."

Luckily for Lori, at that point Ben was looking elsewhere.

In a bare cell and surrounded by interrogators, the man called Corbin paled. "No," he refused. "No, no, no. Absolutely not."

The implacable expression on the chief interrogator's face suggested that such a response was unlikely to be acceptable. "No? But you promised to help us, Corbin. That was the deal."

"I have helped you," protested the prisoner. "I've given you details of the locations of all CHAOS bases, including that one. But I'm an informant, not a tour guide. You can act on your own." A thin smile creased Corbin's mouth. "You seem to have enough men."

"Oh, we do," said the chief interrogator, "and we've been paying little visits to your former colleagues. And we've found precisely what you knew we'd find, Corbin. The agents of CHAOS are either scattered or dead. Nemesis reached your bases before us and destroyed everything, leaving us with no clue as to where in cyberspace it might be lurking, no way to trace it."

"Yes, well, we created Nemesis to be thorough as well as homicidal."

"My problem, Corbin, is that the weeklong deadline that you and your fellow agents gave before the commitment of another atrocity has all but expired, and I'd rather have Nemesis expire, too, before that happens."

Corbin shook his head in weary frustration. "You ask questions but don't listen to the answers. Nemesis is no longer under my control. It is sentient. It makes its own decisions. The deadline we gave is indeed *dead*."

"So," pressed the chief interrogator, "you're saying that Nemesis could strike at any time, is that right?"

"Brain cells at work," Corbin snorted. "Give the man a promotion."

"Which makes it all the more imperative that you accompany us to the final CHAOS base — the base where Nemesis was actually engineered — *and* that you accompany us before another attack takes place."

Corbin saw how he had been outwitted, but he remained unmoved. "You already know my answer to that one."

"In that case," said the chief interrogator to one of his companions, "I think we might return Mr. Corbin to the general prison population. I'm sure he'll be very comfortable in a nice new cell, all computer controlled, with Internet access. We could even add a little VR capacity, just for him. Arrange it."

"All right, all right," Corbin broke in. "I'll go with you, I'll take you there, but I can assure you, we won't find anything.

Nemesis is too clever to be caught so simply. And we travel in low-tech transport only. I want no more experiences like the Light Train." Corbin seemed to think of something else. His eyes narrowed craftily. "And one more condition . . ."

"You're not in a position to make conditions, Corbin."

"Oh, on this one, I am." Corbin smiled sneeringly. "We don't go alone. Those kids, the ones who saved the Light Train, whoever they are, I want them with us. They have a knack for staying alive in unpleasant circumstances. If they're not on your team, chief interrogator, neither am I." Corbin leaned forward and used the man's own words against him. "Arrange it."

It would probably have been better for Ben's health not to be watching Solo Team Spyscaping, but there was no way he'd leave the viewing room now, not unless a number of wild horses suddenly became available and agreed to drag him away.

Simon Macey and his teammates had appropriated the Ankh of Power. They'd beaten off the attack of the mummies ("That about wraps it up," Macey had had the gall to quip). They'd even negotiated their passage to the inner pyramid wall (and nobody dared mention the time, particularly not to Ben). All they needed to do now was solve the hieroglyphic code before they were overwhelmed by mummified reinforcements and access the exit hatch. Then Bond Team's Spyscape — their pride and joy, a cyberspace that upon completion, Ben had suggested confidently, was uncrackable — would not only be cracked but smashed and splintered into disastrous smithereens.

Macey's team was about to take the lead in the race for the Sherlock Shield.

"It's not possible." Ben was already in denial. "The way they waltzed through the pyramid. We spent hours on that maze program. They got through it like it was a one-way street."

"They're not home yet," reminded Cally. "They won't solve my codes so quickly."

She should have added, "I hope." While their teammates held off lumbering mummies with sleepshot, Simon Macey and Sonia Dark tested out combinations of hieroglyphics. A single symbol lit up.

"They've got one!" Jennifer cried.

"One's fine. One's okay," Ben was rationalizing furiously. "One doesn't matter. They need all six."

"Yeah? Well they're halfway there," observed Jake unhappily, as two more hieroglyphics lit up to give Solo Team hope.

Lori didn't know quite what she should be feeling as she looked on. She was loyal to her friends, of course, and to Ben. She wanted Bond Team to win. But as she watched the intense concentration on Simon's face, she felt that she kind of wanted him to win as well. Whichever way it went, Lori thought, perhaps the real loser would be her.

"Four! That's four symbols," Eddie observed. "They only need two more."

"The math is coming along then, Ed," commented Jake.

"Another one," Cally corrected. "But the code was . . . I don't understand."

Nobody dared to say anything when the sixth symbol lit up like a good idea. Solo Team cheered in triumph as the Spyscape program terminated. Nobody needed to consult a timepiece. When you've been beaten, you just know it.

"Understand?" Ben had directed his anger and frustration inward. They infected his words like poison. "Oh, I think I do.

Macey and his crew, they couldn't have done so well so quickly without some kind of help. It's just not possible."

"What?" Lori said, concerned. "You think Simon cheated?"

"Worse than that." Ben regarded the others coldly, clinically. "I think there's a traitor in Bond Team."

CHAPTER TEN

"All right, Macey, who was it?" Ben burst into the virtual-reality chamber.

"Ben, wait!" yelled Lori, with the rest of Bond Team in pursuit.

The hiss of cybercradles opening was still in the air. Simon Macey hadn't even sat up yet, was still wired to the mechanism that transferred the students between realities. He didn't look like he'd be able to sit up, either. Not with Ben practically on top of him, seizing his collar and shouting.

"Who was it, you cheating scumbag? Who sold us out?"

But Simon Macey was laughing, in a spluttering, half-strangled sort of way. Laughing in Ben's face. "Second best hard to take, Stanton? Well, get used to it."

"Ben, let him up. Please." Lori said, pulling at one arm.

Jake was at his other side. "Can't you see this is what he wants? You're playing his game."

"I'd take a step back if I were you, Bond Team." Sonia Dark and the others were already out of their cybercradles. They'd brought the instinct for violence from the Spyscape into the virtual-reality chamber with them. Shaping up for a fight.

"Or what? A step back or what?" Jennifer, for one, seemed more than ready to oblige. "You going to make us?"

"It'll be our pleasure," said Sonia Dark.

"What —" with a voice like a thunderbolt, Corporal Keene asserted his authority — "is going on here?"

"I think you could call it a healthy debate, Corporal," said Eddie.

"Stanton, let go of Macey before I say disciplinary procedures, or you'll find out what they are." Ben, of course, obeyed, but he didn't like it. "That's better. Now somebody answer my question. What is going on here?"

"Stanton tried to kill me, sir," Simon Macey moaned, detaching himself from the cybercradle. "He's a lunatic. Just because we beat them on the Spyscape."

"You didn't beat us," Ben raged. "You cheated. They cheated, Corporal."

"Is that true, Macey?"

"No, sir. Of course not, sir." Simon was the definition of shocked innocent. "We just did our best, like we always do. Stanton's just a bad loser."

"And do you have any evidence of misconduct on Solo Team's part, Stanton?"

Ben hated to say it, but there was no alternative. "No, sir."

"Then there's nothing more to be said, is there? Accept the outcome of the competition with the good grace we expect at Deveraux." Keene pointed a less than graceful finger at Ben and Simon. "Now shake hands before I report you both."

"But, sir . . ." Ben felt he'd rather cut off his hand than use it to touch Simon Macey.

"Shake." Keene was unmoved. "Hands."

Ben did. He clenched Macey's hand like he wanted to crush it into powder. Simon's grip was just as unforgiving. "No hard feelings, Stanton?" Simon sneered, though the eyes of both boys reflected plenty of them. "But I'd calm down if I were you. Be more like Lori. She's the only decent thing about Bond Team."

And that's when Jake saw everything. He saw Lori's eyes flit to Macey at the mention of her name. He saw the color rise to her cheeks. He saw her look away again. Guiltily.

"Jake, do you suppose Ben could be right?" Cally asked. "There couldn't be a traitor on the team, could there? One of us?"

He shook his head firmly. "No. Don't worry about it, Cal."

But he kept watching.

"I'm right. I know I am." Ben prowled the room like a tiger in a cage. "Somebody must have passed information about our Spyscape to Macey. There's no other explanation."

Lori watched him nervously. If she'd ever been meaning to tell Ben about Simon's suggestion of a truce, now was not the time. "But who'd do it, Ben?" she asked, certain that nobody had, and equally sure that Simon would not cheat, though she kept that belief firmly to herself as well. "And what would they hope to gain? Surely we all want the team to do well."

"Maybe Daly?" Ben pondered. "As a way of getting back at me for . . . nah. Stabbing his teammates in the back isn't his style, even I have to admit that."

"Of course it isn't." Lori was genuinely shocked. "How could you even think it?"

"Cally?" Ben was checking team members off on his fingers. "We've had our disagreements in the past."

"That were resolved."

"Maybe Jennifer kind of heard we'd been discussing her behavior, and this is her revenge. Or maybe Eddie . . . nah, it can't be Eddie. That really is ridiculous."

"It's all ridiculous," complained Lori, "and what about me? You haven't accused me yet, Ben. I must be on your list of suspects."

"What are you talking about?" Ben paused in his pacing and regarded Lori with something that seemed like hurt in his expression. "I've never doubted you for a second, Lori, not for less time than that. Why do you think I'm talking to you about this? I trust you. Absolutely. You're my girl."

Lori's cheeks colored, and she hoped that Ben would interpret it as pleasure rather than guilt. "I'm glad to hear it," she said, but there was also hurt in her voice.

Ben sat on the bed beside her and took her hand. "Listen, I've been meaning to say this since we got back from the dome, about the other day, when you called me, you know? I'm sorry. I was short with you. I shouldn't have been. I was wrong."

She didn't hear apologies from Ben very often, admissions of error. Lori felt the need to reciprocate somehow. Maybe now was her chance to say, "I'm sorry, too, particularly as I went off and kissed Simon Macey." On the other hand, perhaps she should try for something a little less shocking. "It's all right, Ben," she said finally. "You were on a mission. I was the one being stupid."

"Makes us a good match then, doesn't it?" Ben grinned. "Stupidity is common. Maybe we should get Eddie and make it a threesome."

"No," she said. "I'm happy with just the two of us."

"Good. Then it's unanimous." He moved to kiss her.

"But, Ben." Lori pressed a finger to his lips. "This business about Solo Team. Tell me you've changed your mind. Tell me you agree there's no traitor."

Ben sighed. "And mean it?" Lori nodded. He sighed again and shrugged defeatedly, in bafflement. "You're right, Lo. I'm wrong again. There's no traitor. Can't be. But —" and this time it was Ben's finger against Lori's lips — "Macey got hold of our Spyscape somehow. I'd put money on it."

"Of course we didn't." Simon staggered. "I want to beat Bond Team, sure, even though you're a member, Lori, but I wouldn't cheat to do it. That's unethical. I mean, in the end, I'd only be cheating our team."

Lori smiled with relief. "I knew as much," she said. "I just wanted to hear you say it."

"Me, I'll say anything you want. So Ben's none too pleased that we've edged ahead, then?" Lori didn't look like she wanted to answer. "It's all right," Simon prompted. "Whatever you say won't go beyond these four walls." In an environment where privacy came at a premium, Spy High's classrooms were often of greater value to its students when they were empty than when full. "Lori?"

"What do you think? We can put the truce idea on ice, at least until after Last Team Standing." Lori looked away from Simon and remembered herself with Ben only a short time ago. "And I think we'd better cool it, too, Simon."

"What? And we were just warming up."

"I'm Ben's girlfriend, Simon. And I want to be."

"You sure?" Simon moved back into Lori's line of vision. "Look me in the eye, Lori." In the smile. "Are you sure? Because you didn't seem so sure about it when we kissed. I mean, it was a *we* kind of kiss, wasn't it? Both of us were in there. Maybe if we tried a repeat performance . . ."

Lori shook her head, although with much less conviction than she'd been hoping to convey. "No, Simon, I —"

"Bond Team to Briefing Room One, please." It was the intercom. "Bond Team to Briefing Room One."

The students paused, frowned. "What's that all about?" asked Simon.

Lori shook her head. "I have no idea, but it means I've got to go, and that's probably just as well."

"I'm not changing the way I feel about you, Lori," Simon said. "I know you feel something for me, too. I'll be waiting. When Ben blows it, you know where to find me."

Lori shifted her weight uncomfortably. "I've got to go."

"I'll be seeing you, Lori," Simon called after her. "Soon."

Lori left the classroom at warp speed, head lowered. She saw Jake's feet just in time to stop herself from colliding with him. Her cry was more in case he should glance past her into the room and observe Simon Macey than for any fear that she might cause him an injury. "Jake," she dreaded. "What are you doing here?"

"Looking for you," he said simply. "Seems we've got a briefing to attend."

"I know." Lori grabbed Jake's hand and pulled. "So what are we waiting for?"

She was lucky. Jake followed her and didn't look where she didn't want him to look. *Panic over*, Lori thought.

Unfortunately for her, Jake didn't need to see Simon Macey in the flesh. He'd already heard quite enough.

It was like one of those old war films his dad used to watch on Twentieth Century Gold, Eddie thought. Paratroopers flown in deep behind enemy lines on an ultrasecret mission, parachutes strapped on and sitting in two rows staring at each other from either side of the plane, chewing gum and looking mean. Only instead of a plane, Bond Team was crammed into the back of a truck that had probably seen service in World War II — everything was low-tech, to prevent Nemesis from snooping — and there wasn't a paratrooper in sight. They had to make do with some equally hard-bitten army types brought along by Keene and arranged opposite the teenagers, wearing looks that were so mean that Eddie didn't dare catch their eye in case they should take offense and liven up the journey by disemboweling him with their teeth. Keene sat opposite, too, or at least a working statue of him. The man with the head of a weasel, introduced as the Chief Interrogator, was up front, with the driver and the guy who was responsible for them all being there in the first place (wherever "there" actually was), the former agent of CHAOS now known as Corbin.

Yes, the likelihood of Eddie being fried by a psychotic computer virus before bedtime was all down to Corbin.

"Of course," the voice of Jonathan Deveraux had said as his face regarded Bond Team from the screen in Briefing Room One, "your participation is completely voluntary. Corporal Keene and a platoon of handpicked men will accompany you, but even so, this operation brings with it significant risk. That cannot be denied."

And significant glory, Eddie could almost see Ben thinking. Significant opportunity to make up for the Spyscapes.

"We understand, sir," Ben said in a noble leader sort of way. "We want to go."

"That's right," Jake echoed.

Eddie wondered why, until he remembered the dome — Jake's dome — and the destruction that everyone, minus himself and Lori, had witnessed firsthand. Back when he'd been sidelined. Again. "We're ready, Mr. Deveraux, sir," he'd said, though it seemed the room had suddenly gone deaf.

So here they were. Eddie peered out through the flapping tarpaulin at the back of the truck. He glimpsed ragged trees, a dirt road, nowhere in particular. "Why can't the villains' headquarters ever be anywhere they put in travel brochures?" he muttered. The truck jolted beneath him. "Or at least with decent roads. I feel like I've just done twelve rounds with a Swedish masseur."

"Eddie," said Cally wearily, "do the words *shut* and *up* mean anything to you?"

"More and more each day," grumbled Eddie, wondering how much more interminable the journey could get. Even an attack by Nemesis would be preferable to death by boredom.

The truck braked. The statue of Keene suddenly became animated and barked orders that only those with a military function seemed able to understand. The soldiers clambered out of the truck all at once. "Can't wait for their welcome cocktail," observed Eddie.

"Come on." Ben ushered his teammates. "We must have arrived."

It didn't look promising. The road had petered out, and in its place, a large mound rose before them, like a hill with stunted growth.

"Am I missing something here?" Eddie wondered. "Can CHAOS HQ only be seen with X-ray vision?"

"All right, Corbin," the chief interrogator was warning, "no tricks."

Turning his head slightly to acknowledge the presence of Bond Team, Corbin walked over to a nearby tree, pressed his palm against the trunk, and pushed in. At once, the mound began to split open, like a mouth smiling a dark and secret smile. The turf and the soil — they were grafted to steel. They became doors. And beyond the doors, a passage, like the entrance to a crypt. Suddenly, being stuck in the truck didn't seem so bad to Eddie.

The same thought had apparently also occurred to Corbin. "There," he informed the chief interrogator. "I've done what I said I'd do. You can find your own way from here. I'll wait in the truck."

The chief interrogator chuckled. "The transport stays where it is, Corbin. You don't," he said. "Please." He indicated the gaping fissure in the earth. "After you."

It was conceivable at that point that Corbin might have made a break for it had Keene's men not been training their automatic weapons directly on him. He smiled thinly, humorlessly. "As if they'll be of any use if Nemesis finds us." Soldiers or guns, he didn't specify.

Reluctantly, he moved toward the CHAOS stronghold. "I want the kids close to me. They've seen what this thing can do."

"Don't worry, Corbin," Jake promised, sounding more like a threat. "We'll be right behind you. For the sake of Dome Thirteen."

Corbin led the way into the complex, Bond Team and the chief interrogator behind him, all of them flanked by Keene and his men, two of whom the corporal posted at the entrance. "Just in case we need to make a run for it?" Lori whispered to Ben.

The darkness of the crypt claimed them.

Flashlights clicked into life on the soldiers' helmets and weapons. The civilian members of the party carried their own, all except Corbin, who seemed to know where he was going even without the benefit of artificial light. Beams of white stabbed into the black, hinting at the presence of hulks of metal — machinery, perhaps, or raw materials — suggesting deep recesses of darkness, unknowable pits and caves where anything could lurk. Eddie found himself hoping that Keene's soldiers were mean in more than just expression.

"Wait!" Cally called.

Everybody stopped and bunched up. The tension could almost be tasted behind the spikes of light. "What is it?" demanded Keene.

"I thought I saw something, out there, something moving in the dark." But she no longer sounded convinced. "I thought . . . it looked like a man."

Corbin laughed hollowly. "There's nothing moving in here but us, nothing alive anyway. There can't be. Nemesis doesn't leave loose ends behind."

"Keep moving, Corbin," Keene instructed.

"But I saw it, I'm sure," Cally breathed, more to herself than to Lori, who squeezed her arm encouragingly. "It was a man, pale as death."

"The sooner we get out of here the better," Jennifer muttered. The darkness was too much like in her dreams. If it wasn't for the others, for Jake being there, she'd probably be screaming by now. And unable to stop.

"End of the road," said Corbin, approaching a slab of solid blackness before him. The flashlights revealed a steel wall and a door. "The main labs are through here."

"Then get us in there." The chief interrogator seemed eager.

"I don't think so." Corbin shook his head finally. "The door's scanner is activated. It won't recognize your signature."

"It's not our fingerprints it'll be reading."

"Oh, no. No." For the first time Corbin seemed genuinely fearful. "If I use mine and Nemesis is watching, then we're dead. No. If I activate this door, I'm killing us all. You can't make me do it!"

"Keene," said the chief interrogator. "Show Mr. Corbin that we can."

Keene gestured. Two soldiers grabbed Corbin and forced his left hand against a control panel on the wall. "No! No! You mustn't!" The man's desperate, almost childish pleas dropped into the darkness like pebbles into a pond. There was a slight ripple of sound, and then silence. "You've killed us," Corbin sobbed. "You've killed us all!"

Bond Team looked at each other with uncertainty. If it had been anybody but Corbin, they might have been sympathetic.

The lab door slid open.

"Keep hold of him," the chief interrogator instructed the soldiers. "Now, let's see what we can see." He stepped through the doorway.

Corbin twisted in his captors' grasp to face Bond Team. "You know what's going to happen now, don't you?" His terrified gaze flitted between them. "It'll be like the train. We're rats in a trap. Nemesis knows. You understand me? Nemesis is *here.*"

But it didn't seem so. Nothing living seemed to have been in the lab for a long time. There were banks of computers, rows of control panels, strange technological constructions whose original purpose could only be guessed, but there was not a flicker

of electronic activity to any of them. They were all smashed, ruined, wrecked. They were debris. It was as if a bomb had been
detonated in the heart of the lab. Only a faint, faded light lin-
gered in the air, like a ghost. It was at least sufficient for the
flashlights to be turned off. The members of Bond Team returned theirs to their belt pouches.

"Looks like it was one hell of a party," said Eddie. "Kind of
glad I wasn't invited." The others looked as though they felt the
same.

"So this is where Nemesis was born." The chief interrogator's voice sounded thin and temporary in the lab. "Let's see if we
can find anything we can use. Corbin, with me. I want to know
if we can get any of these machines up and running."

Keene and his soldiers — apart from the two who had man-
handled Corbin before and who now seemed permanently assigned to be within grabbing distance of him — spread out to
further explore the lab's dark corners and distant doorways,
shunning what feeble light there was.

Corbin turned again to Bond Team as if it could provide
some kind of last chance for him. "Listen, you kids," he urged,
"I'm relying on you. Talk to him. He has no idea what'll happen
to us if we stay here. There's no point in us staying. Nemesis has
destroyed everything, you can see that. You can see that, can't
you?"

"All I can see is a loser who'd have destroyed us if he could,"
said Jake, "and who nearly destroyed my family. Our hearts
bleed for you, Corbin."

"You. Computer girl," he said to Cally. "You know what I'm
talking about, don't you? You've stopped Nemesis once. It won't
forget that. It'll want you. It'll hunt you down."

"Yeah?" Cally met Corbin's desperate gaze coolly. "But I bet it'll go after you first." She hoped her teammates didn't see her shudder. She remembered the digital eyes downloading hate, the cybernetic fangs, the computer *knowing* who she was.

"Sir? Sir! Over here!" One of the soldiers had found something.

Or somebody.

They rushed to his side, encircling a form that had gone unnoticed beneath a collapsed console. The man's lab coat was shredded like bandages, his other clothes the same. Wires like anorexic snakes wound around his limbs and chest, like ropes binding his body together. More wires noosed his neck and webbed their way over his scalp, his skull.

"What does this mean, Corbin?" demanded the chief interrogator.

Corbin's head shook like a sudden seizure. "I don't know. I don't . . . it's Patten, one of the virsus's . . . fathers . . ."

"Was." The chief interrogator knelt by the body. "He's not anything now apart from dead. But what about this?" The chief interrogator's inquisitive fingers followed the trail of the wires over the dead man's head. They seemed to have burrowed into his skull. The hair was scorched away in several places and the skin blackened and burned. "Corbin. What's been going on here?"

The chief interrogator raised his head, exposing his Adam's apple as it bobbed in his nervous throat. The dead man's arms shot up like pistons; dead hands clamped around his neck like twin vises. Dead fingers squeezed, powered by more than flesh and blood.

The chief interrogator would not be asking anymore questions.

"Get back!" Ben cried, yanking Lori with him.

Weapons riddled the disturbingly active body. To a corpse, laser fire made no difference. Patten got up.

"What did I tell you?" Corbin screamed. "We're all going to die!"

"Keep together," Ben hissed to his teammates. "Watch each other's backs."

"You've got it," gritted Jack.

A cry rang out from one of the other rooms. Then a second. Two bursts of laser fire. Brief. Two soldiers had gone in. Two dead scientists came out, bristling with wires like Patten.

Wires like a puppeteer's strings.

"Nemesis," gasped Cally. "It's controlling them."

"Time to go?" suggested Eddie.

But now the shadows were moving and closing in. The dead scientists of CHAOS reached for the intruders with pale hands.

"We're surrounded!" someone shouted.

"One hell of a party," groaned Eddie.

CHAPTER ELEVEN

"Fire at will!" Keene yelled. "Take them out!"

Laser blasts pulsed toward the advancing zombie scientists. The hail of fire staggered them, made them sway as if facing a strong wind. It slowed them down, but it didn't stop them. The dead kept on coming.

"Form a defensive circle!" snapped Keene. To Bond Team he commanded, "Stay behind us. Stay in the circle."

"Makes me feel a lot better," Eddie grunted. "Anybody remember Custer's Last Stand? Anybody got a plan?"

"How about don't let 'em grab you, for a start?" said Jake.

But in an enclosed space, avoiding the homicidal hands of the zombies was easier said than done. The soldier in front of Jennifer was evidently not used to an enemy that would not behave and fall down when shot. He was losing his discipline, being drawn forward, breaking the circle. He was focusing so exclusively on one target that he failed to take account of the others. So they took account of him instead, seizing his arms, twisting them like plasticene, ending the soldier's cries of frustration and fear forever.

Jennifer braced herself as they turned toward her, but they didn't seem to notice, didn't seem to care. The zombies had sightless eyes for only one member of Bond Team, and they began to press toward her. Cally.

"Oh, no, you don't, Mr. Dead!" Jake swung a metal chair at a zombie's head. The blow shattered its neck and left the head dangling limply, loosely, eyes to the floor. The murderous arms flailed wildly.

And now the uneven battle was well and truly in effect. Soldiers and scientists struggled hand to hand, life to death. The integrity of the circle was broken. There was chaos.

"Bond Team, to me!" Keene tried to protect his students, but Patten seemed to have other ideas and grappled with the corporal, hands like iron seeking his neck. Only a laser burst at point-blank range jolted the dead man sufficiently for Keene to escape his clutches.

"Think ninja program," Ben instructed his teammates. "Avoid and deflect. Don't let them touch you."

"They've got one weakness," Lori added. "They're slow. We're fast. Make it count."

Zombie hands lunged. Martial-arts techniques knocked them away. Lori was right. If they moved quickly enough and improvised, they could keep at least a temporary advantage. Being dead seemed to slow your reaction time. Bond Team struck out, well-aimed sweeps with their legs sending their attackers crashing awkwardly to the floor, their fists and forearms blocking assault after assault. But all the time, growing weaker. And one by one, the soldiers fell.

"Cally!" Jennifer tried to make herself heard above the cries and clamor. "They want Cally!"

"I didn't know I was so popular," Cally observed, dodging and then kicking to send her newest assailant toppling, "but I could use a little help here."

Bond Team closed ranks.

"Nemesis knows you're the biggest threat," Jake realized.

"You stopped it on the train. It thinks you might be able to stop it now."

"And Cal," moaned Eddie, a flurry of blows beating back a zombie, "we kind of hope so, too." Dead fingers brushed his shoulder. "And make it quick, all right?"

Corbin didn't plan on waiting. His fear had turned into cunning, the survival instinct of the trapped animal. When the two soldiers guarding him became embroiled in the more pressing matter of saving their own lives, he saw his chance. Only for a moment, the ebb and flow of conflict had opened a path to the lab door. Corbin darted for it.

He scarcely expected to get there, but he did. Now he could turn the tables on the lot of them, his deceased former comrades, those brainless soldiers, those annoying kids, all of them. "Corbin!" The corporal shouted after him. Well, let him shout. Use the old vocal chords while he could, before they were ripped out like string. Corbin waved farewell as he slipped out of the lab.

The door was fingerprint activated. He'd told them that. And he'd warned them, too, but they forced him to open it. Nobody had to force him to close it again. Everyone else would stay inside.

But what about him? Not safe yet. Plenty of darkness out here for the dead to hide in. Not safe yet.

Corbin raced toward the distant prospect of freedom and the outside world. Ahead of him were the wide open doors of the complex itself and a light at the end of a particularly unsettling tunnel.

At every gasping, whimpering, heart- and foot-pounding yard of the way, Corbin expected white hands to thrust out of the darkness, grab him, twist him, and break him into pieces. But it didn't happen. Nemesis must have concentrated its effort on the lab itself. Almost howling with elated relief, Corbin burst out into reassuring sunlight and the blithe trill of birdsong.

The absence of the soldiers that Keene had posted at the complex's entrance did not seem to occur to Corbin. There was room in his agitated mind for one thought only.

The truck. Because the truck meant escape. The truck meant safety.

He hugged himself with delight. There was the truck. Here he was clambering into the driver's seat. There were the keys, conveniently still in the ignition. Not that he'd need the keys. He could have hotwired the truck. He was Corbin, agent of CHAOS. He could do anything. He turned the key: The truck's engine fired on the first try. Maybe he'd even relaunch the organization, this time with himself as undisputed leader, of course. He was alive, and he was safe. Anything was possible.

Only next time there wouldn't be a Nemesis. Too dangerous. Too unpredictable. He wondered whether those strange, intense kids were dead yet. No, next time there'd be no mistakes — and no loose ends.

Like the soldiers at the entrance. Corbin remembered them now. Where had they gone?

Maybe in the truck. Maybe that was them moving about behind him.

The sweat on his skin turned to ice.

Maybe it wasn't.

Corbin froze. He didn't dare look behind him.

Until a pair of dead, white hands seized his head and turned it around for him. All the way around.

* * *

They couldn't last much longer. Cally knew it as well as the others, as well as the soldiers who were being overwhelmed by their apparently unstoppable assailants with increasing regularity. The shrinking band of survivors' backs were against the wall — literally as well as figuratively. Even the zombies seemed to sense that their triumph was only a matter of time.

If only they could break that control, Cally thought, *disrupt it somehow.* But *somehow* wasn't going to be good enough. If only she had time to plan, to come up with an idea. But time wasn't on their side, either.

"Cal!" someone shouted.

Behind her. She wheeled but hands like cold meat were on her, clamping around her throat. It was Patten, forcing her down. She couldn't dislodge him.

"Help me!" Cally choked out her appeal. "Some . . . one . . . help . . ."

Patten squeezed at her throat as if she were a tube of toothpaste. She heard her neck cracking.

"Some . . . one . . ." The world was turning dark.

And then came a message for her from beyond the grave. It was Patten's voice, but the words of someone else: "Organic . . . forms . . . im . . . pure . . ."

And there seemed to be a gleam of sadistic pleasure in the scientist's eyes, those staring zombie eyes now only inches away from her own. A gleam that throbbed and pulsated like a yellow heartbeat. And not *in* the eyes, either, but *behind* them. Behind them.

No way could Cally afford to die now. The others were relying on her.

She clung to consciousness like a drowning man to a life preserver. Keene — was it Keene? — was battering Patten's skull to no avail, splintering it like a tree trunk. "Eyes," Cally croaked. "Behind the eyes . . . shoot . . ."

Keene got the point. There was a blinding flash by her face and a savage thunder of noise. Patten jolted backward, his capacity for vision reduced by one-half. He released his hold, and Cally gasped for air. Through the hole where his eyeballs had been, brains and circuits mingled uselessly. Dead again.

"Control chip," Cally coughed. "That's the answer."

"The eyes!" Keene cried out, like Archimedes inspired. "Aim for the eyes!"

As if they understood the corporal's words, and maybe they did, Patten's fellow zombies momentarily paused, almost seemed to glance at each other for advice. The surviving soldiers didn't pause, momentarily or otherwise. They took aim. They fired. Eyeballs popped like champagne corks.

And the zombies fell, as if struck by a sudden desire to be buried, a sudden realization that the dead had no right to be attacking the living like this. As if the puppets' strings had suddenly been snipped.

A roar of hope from the remaining humans. The tide was turning.

"Great shooting, guys," admired Eddie. "Looks like you win the whole row of Kewpie dolls."

"Cal, are you okay?" Jennifer and Jake were kneeling by her, helping her into a sitting position.

"I've been better," she managed hoarsely.

"You've done well, Cross," Keene approved. "All of you. I think we have the situation well in hand now."

The lab floor was littered with the bodies of the zombies, not to mention the chief interrogator and the majority of Keene's men.

"Hey, Corbin's gone," Ben realized. "And he's shut us in."

"Don't worry, Stanton," said Keene. "He won't get far."

"Neither will we, Corporal," Ben pointed out. "We need Corbin's fingerprints to open the door."

"Ben . . . it's all right . . ." Cally's throat felt like it had just gone through a cheese grater. "The other scientists . . . must have had access . . . too."

"The other scientists?"

Cally indicated the heaps of white-lab-coated bodies. "Take . . . your pick."

It was a weary and generally disheartened Bond Team who finally returned with Corporal Keene to Spy High. They'd found Corbin's corpse in the truck, as well as two others who'd had to come eye to eye with a laser bolt in order to remind them of the fact that they were already dead. But the entire ill-fated expedition to CHAOS's last laboratory complex had not yielded any significant new intelligence nor granted any hint as to how to locate and eliminate Nemesis. All it had attained was the loss of lives.

"That's the risk we all take in this line of work," Keene said on the journey home. "Be grateful they weren't yours." Eddie wondered why the corporal didn't go for a second career in motivational speaking.

"Shower and sleep," Ben groaned, as the members of Bond Team ached their way toward their rooms. "Or maybe both at the same time."

"Think I could go for a snack or something first," said Jennifer. "Anyone care to join me? Jake?" With pointed hopefulness.

Jake seemed torn. "No, I don't think so, Jen. Sorry. Think I'll just turn in as well."

"Oh." Jennifer tried hard to mask her disappointment but wondered, if Jake really liked her as much as Cally said he did, wouldn't he have said yes in order to spend time with her? "Okay. It doesn't matter." The others didn't seem interested, either. "Just me, then."

"Nah, can't have that. I'll keep you company, Jen," Eddie volunteered.

"Great, Eddie. Thanks." Jennifer saw Cally raise her eyebrows sympathetically. And it may have been tiredness or stress blurring her vision, but just as she and Eddie left the others to make for the rec room, Jennifer thought she also saw Jake lightly touching Lori's shoulder, softly whispering something in her ear. But she must have imagined that. *What would Jake want with Lori that seemed so secretive?*

Lori asked herself the same question after lying to Ben and Cally that she and Jake had decided to grab a snack after all. They never got as far as the rec room. The study rooms at Deveraux were as effective as grounds for confrontations as they were elevators.

"Well, Mr. Secret and Urgent?" Lori could tell that something was bothering Jake. "What's the matter? This isn't like you, Jake."

"Consorting with the enemy isn't like you either, Lori, but it's happening, isn't it?"

"What? What do you mean?" For several seconds of disbelieving silence on Jake's part, Lori really couldn't guess. Her definition of *enemy* took a while to expand far enough to include Simon Macey. But when it did, she knew exactly what Jake meant. She was in trouble. "I don't understand," she bluffed awkwardly. "Maybe I'd better just . . ." Lori headed for the door.

"Simon Macey," said Jake, stopping her in her tracks as if the words were some sort of paralysis spell. "Tell me about you and Simon Macey, Lori."

"Jake?" Lori half-turned toward him, but didn't trust a direct gaze. "There isn't a me and Simon Macey. How could there be?"

"I don't know, Lori," mused Jake, "but there I was thinking Ben had gone off the deep end again with all of his rantings about a traitor in the team, you know, just as a kind of cover-up story to excuse the fact that we'd been beaten for once, and there I was, more than half expecting our noble leader to accuse me of being in league with Macey, and then, what do I discover?" his voice became colder, flintier. "There is a traitor after all, and it's not me. It's you, Lori."

"I'm not a traitor, Jake." Lori's blue eyes flashed denial at the accusation. "You're wrong."

Jake sighed, "I saw your reaction after the Spyscaping. I heard you with Macey in the classroom before we went off with Keene."

Lori shook her head. "I don't know what you're talking about."

"I'm not imaginative enough to make this up," Jake persisted. "I mean, I heard what you said, the both of you. He's not changing the way he feels. He knows you feel something for him, too. I mean, tell me I'm making this up."

"You're making it up." But she spoke to the floor.

"So you haven't been secretly seeing Simon Macey? Haven't

been passing him information about our Spyscape and who knows what else?"

"No. No. And no. You're wrong, Jake." But her body language said he was right. "And I think we're finished here."

"I could have gone straight to Ben with this." Jake tried a different approach. "I could have told him without speaking to you, Lori. Doesn't that suggest something? I only want to help. Ben's right about one thing. You can't trust Simon Macey."

You can, Lori thought. *If only the others realized that.* "I don't need any help, Jake."

He was losing her. She was at the door. "I could still do it," he warned. "I could go and tell Ben right now. Is that what you want, Lori?"

"You do whatever you want," she said. And she closed the door behind her.

So why didn't he, then? Go to Ben. It'd be a crushing blow to Stanton's ego, learning that the girlfriend, whose loyalty and talents he'd been boasting about to Jake before, was in fact the traitor and in Simon Macey's pocket, if not elsewhere. It'd be a rich revenge for all of Ben's insults.

But revenge wouldn't help the team, wouldn't boost morale. Revenge was for the bitter. He couldn't tell Ben or anyone else, even though it was obvious Lori was lying. But Jake couldn't quite bring himself to believe that she was cold-bloodedly selling them out, either. Not Lori. She was too — he groped for the right word — *good.*

Still, he couldn't let the matter rest like this. He had to do something.

Jake sighed. Seemed his bed would have to wait a while yet.

* * *

Eddie and Ben were sound asleep. It'd probably take Nemesis smashing through the wall to make either of them stir, and then they'd be more likely to turn over on their other side. Even so, Jake applied the clingskin as quietly as possible, then whispered the window open as wide as it would go.

He didn't want to put his foot through the glass on his way out.

Not as sheer as the Wall, not actually moving like the Light Train, clingskinning up and down the exterior of Deveraux Academy was going to be a breeze. Jake kept his concentration level high, however. Falling three floors into the shrubbery would be an embarrassing way to break your neck.

He slithered along the wall between the rows of windows, keeping well out of range of anyone who was still up and might want to take an admiring peek at the night. Lovers, maybe. Or conspirators.

Jake knew the location of Simon Macey's room. He counted the number of windows along from his own. Didn't want to snoop on just anybody. When he'd activated his belt recorder and inserted his earpiece, he was no longer certain he even wanted to eavesdrop on Simon Macey. The mic on the belt recorder could capture the sound of a heartbeat through a concrete wall three feet thick. It brought the slobbering sounds of Macey and Sonia Dark too distressingly close for comfort. Still, he supposed he ought to count his blessings: At least he didn't have to watch.

Jake shifted his weight and would have sighed had the making of any sound while clinging to a wall outside someone's window not been a bad idea. He was wasting his time. He'd hoped that if the room was empty, he'd have been able to slip in and find evidence of Macey's involvement with Lori — some proof to challenge her with. Alternately, he'd hoped that he'd catch Macey saying something incriminating, thinking he was safe from prying ears. Neither possibility was working out, and if he had to listen to Simon and Sonia's game of tonsil hockey for very much longer, his dinner would be vacating his stomach.

Relief at last. Permanent, Jake prayed. Macey was laughing, the way con artists must do when they trick old ladies. "What's so funny?" Sonia Dark asked him. It was Jake's question, too.

"Just thinking of Stanton's expression again. Priceless. If it was a photograph, I'd have it framed."

"Really?" Sonia Dark didn't sound entirely impressed. "Sometimes, Simon, I think your rivalry with Ben Stanton is more important to you than I am."

"Then sometimes you're wrong, babe."

No making up, Jake begged silently. *Please, no making up.*

"Really?" Sonia repeated, unconvinced. "Well I think you're taking too great an interest in Lori Angel." Maybe Jake's little clingskin excursion wasn't going to be a total loss, after all. "I know what you said, but it looks to me like you're beginning to enjoy being with her."

"I am," Simon admitted, "as long as she's useful to us. I mean, getting her password for the Spyscapes was brilliant, wasn't it? Bit of a sneak preview didn't do us any harm, did it? And there'll be more to come yet, plenty more information that I'll be able to squeeze out of her."

"It's the squeezing part that worries me."

"It shouldn't." A wet slap of a kiss. Jake wondered if he'd heard enough. "We all have to make sacrifices for the cause, and mine is having to tolerate a brainless bimbo like Lori. But don't worry. It'll only be until after Last Team Standing, then I think someone had better tell Stanton exactly what his precious blue-eyed babe has been up to, don't you? All in the spirit of sportsmanship and unity, of course."

More laughter. Jake almost preferred the smooching.

"So you really don't like her, Simon?"

"Didn't I just say that? All right, one more time."

It was probably just as well that Simon Macey couldn't see Jake's expression during the "one more time." He wouldn't have slept that night. Jake's anger was cold inside him — an iceberg. Macey was more of a sleaze than he could have predicted. Lori was being manipulated, and she didn't even know it. He obviously couldn't tell Ben. It was up to him to do something about the situation.

The only question was what.

CHAPTER TWELVE

Today was the day. She couldn't wait any longer. She had to be sure. After all, what advice had Cally given her? "All you've got to do about it is go up to him and say hi. . . . Talk to him. Tell him how you feel." It was advice that Jennifer finally felt ready to take. The dreams still haunted her sleep, prowled her nights, but they were less painful now, as always was the case once the anniversary had passed for another year. Her mind was clearer, and she was able to give thought to other dreams — the future instead of the past. She, Jake, and the others had survived a second encounter with Nemesis. They'd been given time off from their studies to recover from the ordeal at the CHAOS complex. So the timing was perfect. There wouldn't be a better opportunity.

Today was the day.

Lori and Cally had already left their room before Jennifer had built her courage sufficiently to follow their example. She didn't feel like breakfast. She didn't feel like much of anything until she'd established once and for all if there was a Jennifer and Jake on the emotional horizon. She made straight for the boys' room, knocked, and hoped Jake would answer. He'd answer, and she'd say hi and he'd know what she meant and he'd say hi back and they'd be together and they'd talk . . .

"Lori, is that . . . ?" The door opened. "Jennifer?"

"Ben?" And he was still in his pajamas.

Two disappointed and slightly puzzled members of Bond Team stared at each other.

"Sorry, I was expecting Lori." Ben grinned sheepishly. "We said we'd . . . you know, spend some quality time. Kind of, like, together. Is she still . . . ?" He thumbed vaguely toward the girls' accommodation wing.

"Actually, no," said Jennifer. "I haven't seen her." And why did that single statement of fact suddenly seem suspicious?

"Oh, okay." Ben didn't seem to mind. "Are you . . . did you . . . ?"

"Jake," Jennifer announced. "Can I see Jake?"

"What for?" Was that a knowing grin? Was Ben teasing her?

"What, I need to fill out a form or something before I can see a teammate?" If he was teasing, he'd soon be doing it with a bloody nose.

"No," said Ben curiously, "but you'll need pretty good eyes if you want to see him from there. Jake's not here. It's just me, I'm afraid."

"Oh." *Don't give up,* Jennifer forced herself. *Today is the day.* "Do you know where . . . ?"

Ben shook his head. "Sorry, no idea. I'd invite you in to wait for him, Jen, but I need to get dressed before Lori comes."

"Sure," Jennifer said. "You don't want to put her off."

So not a good start. She wandered along the corridors. Jake not around, and no Lori, either, as if that meant something. Maybe they were eating breakfast. Separately, she hoped, or at the same table but only because they were members of the same team and not because they were holding hands or anything.

She was right. They weren't holding hands. But they were together. With a sudden intake of breath, Jennifer saw them from the window — Lori and Jake, on the grounds outside the school.

It was like a mime show or a silent movie. He was being earnest with her, urging, pleading. His hands wanting to touch her. She was shaking her head, trying to ignore him, looking away. Until he said something else and there was a moment of total stillness. Until he ended it by resting his hands tenderly on her shoulders. Until she nodded and accepted him, tearfully. Until they moved off together, and Jennifer could not see where they went.

It *had* been like a mime show or a silent movie, the kind of entertainment that required no words to communicate meaning. Jennifer interpreted for herself. This was the last time she'd listen to Cally's advice. So much for today being the day. The only day that truly mattered in Jennifer's life had been years ago, and its consequences were still being worked out within her. The thought of Jake had been a distraction from them, a delusion. A promise broken like all of the others.

She'd go to the hologym on her own. Combat program. Preparation. She'd fight.

She didn't need Jake anyway.

Jennifer Chen didn't need anybody.

Eddie dug his toes into the white sand, stretched lavishly, and luxuriated in the blazing Caribbean sun. "This is the life, isn't it, Cal?" He rolled onto his side and winked at Cally, who was spread out on the beach alongside him. She didn't deny it. Eddie let his gaze wander over the perfect palm-fringed bay, the clear, calm waters of the sea sparkled invitingly just a few feet away, and there wasn't another human being in sight. He and Cally had paradise all to themselves. "As good as the real thing.

Only problem is, you don't get to take your tan back into the real world with you."

"I can live with it," said Cally, with her eyes closed.

"You're sounding better today," Eddie remarked. "No long-term injury to the voice then?"

"Apparently not," Cally replied, "though if you keep going on, the same might not apply to my ears."

"Sorry." Eddie rolled onto his back again, squinting at the sky through his sunglasses. "Peace and quiet, rest and relaxation, that's what this leisure program's all about. Thought you'd like it. That's why I suggested you join me, Cal."

"I'm grateful. Really."

"Actually —" this time, Eddie sat up, hunched forward, and cast a faintly embarrassed glance in Cally's direction — "to be honest with you, that wasn't the only reason."

Cally opened her eyes. "If you're thinking about any funny business, *don't*. Skinny-dipping's out for a start."

"No." Eddie sounded hurt. "Nothing like that. Though we did have a good time at Christmas, didn't we? I mean, I know I did."

"I know you did, too," Cally grunted, "but Christmas was a one-off, Eddie. Compliments of the season. Nothing serious. I thought we both realized that. I like you as a friend, but —"

"Forget about the *but*," Eddie said. "Friend is good enough, 'cause what I really wanted to do this morning was to talk to you. As a friend."

"Yeah?" Intrigued, Cally sat up, too. First Jennifer, now Eddie. Seemed like she was kick-starting a career as Bond Team's agony aunt. "Okay, you have my undivided attention. Shoot."

"Do you think I pull my weight in this team?"

Cally considered. "It depends. How much do you weigh?"

"No, I mean seriously." Eddie sighed and shrugged like someone defeated. "That's exactly what I mean. You don't take me seriously, no one does. Why does everyone treat me like the team idiot?"

"Because you're always acting like it?" Cally suggested. "It's the way you come across, Eddie, you must know that. More like a stand-up comedian than a secret agent."

"So you don't think I am pulling my weight?"

"I didn't say that. It's just your personality."

"Great. Just my personality." Eddie frowned forlornly. "You know, when we signed up for Deveraux, I was sure I was going to make my mark. I was going to be the spy with the smile. And since then, I've come so far behind in every class that my marks'll soon start coming back wearing pants. I've been excess when it came to fighting Frankenstein and left behind to twiddle my thumbs while the rest of you took off to Jake's dome. Seems to me like it's too much smile and not enough spy."

"You're being a bit hard on yourself, aren't you?" Cally raised her sunglasses and regarded Eddie sympathetically. "Listen, I didn't think that I fitted in too well at Spy High last term. Ben, in particular, was giving me a bad time, remember? But you've got to have faith in yourself, in your abilities. Doubt's natural. It's how you get through it that makes you strong. And for what it's worth, I like you just the way you are. I wouldn't want you to change at all."

"No?" Eddie seemed to cheer up a little. "Not even a bit more muscle on the old biceps?"

Cally grinned. "There's enough intensity on the team from some of the others. We need a joker in the pack, someone who can keep us sane when the world seems to be falling apart. That's your job, and nobody does it as well as you."

"Ah, you're just saying that."

False modesty now. Eddie was rapidly approaching normal again. Cally thought she'd give him one last encouragement. "No, it's the truth. And you might not believe this either, but when we're in danger, there's no one I'd sooner have at my back."

"Yeah? Well I'm pretty cool with you being at my front, too. Maybe we could kind of practice some positioning now, 'cause in this place, you never know when we might need to go into action."

"Down, tiger," laughed Cally. "I think we're pretty safe here, unless a couple of ninjas go AWOL from the combat programs."

In the distance, far beyond the blue horizon, there was a flicker and a rumble.

"Sounds like they heard you."

"It's just a storm."

Blackness spilled like an oil slick across the sky, tainting and polluting.

"Yeah, well I've got a bit of a problem with that, Cal," Eddie said, removing his sunglasses and dropping them by his side. "There aren't supposed to be any storms in this program, not even a drop of rain." He got to his feet, warily gazing out to a sea that was no longer calm, no longer tranquil.

"So what do you call that?" Cally joined him and rested a hand on his shoulder.

Darkness billowed toward them.

"I call it *trouble*," said Eddie.

* * *

"We all have to make sacrifices for the cause, and mine is having to tolerate a brainless bimbo like Lori."

Lori winced, ashen-faced. Each word was like a slap in the face. Simon's voice might have been reduced in volume now that it was being issued from Jake's belt recorder, but its impact was as great as if he were bellowing in her ear.

"Brainless bimbo . . ."

The worst thing was, he was right. She'd been so easy to deceive, to dupe. The smile. It hadn't been real. Lori hung her head in shame and humiliation.

". . . worry. It'll only be until after Last Team Standing, then . . ."

"Jake, please," Lori pleaded, meekly, defeatedly. "No more."

Jake clicked off the recorder and slotted it back onto his belt. "Talk to me," he said. "How did it happen?"

Lori sighed deeply. She gazed out of the window, her expression distant and lost. "Simon approached me after you'd gone to the dome," she admitted. "He was charming, attentive. He made me feel important, valued, and I've always wanted to feel that, Jake, I need to feel valued. And Ben leaving me behind like he did, taking Jennifer . . . I guess I was a little insecure. I let my defenses down. And he started by assuring me that he wanted to make peace between our two teams. And I believed him. I believed everything he said, even though Ben had told me to watch him. How gullible is that? Makes you want to laugh, doesn't it?"

"I'm not laughing," Jake said, "and I'm not blaming you, either. Wanting to see the best in people, that's better than wanting to see the worst."

Lori's lips twitched with feeling and bitterness. "Better for who? So anyway, you've found the traitor. Ben was right all along. Thanks to me, we can probably say good-bye to the Sherlock Shield, and I can certainly say good-bye to a boyfriend. Ben's not going to find this easy to forgive."

Jake cast Lori a look, then followed it up more positively. "Ben doesn't have to know."

"What do you mean? You're not going to tell him?"

"Why would I tell him? What good would that do?"

"But what about Simon? What's to stop him . . . ?"

Jake dismissed the idea. "He's not going to be telling Ben anything while he thinks you don't know the truth. You heard him on the tape. Our friend Simon's not finished with you yet."

"Oh, yes, he is," Lori suddenly blazed, her dismay finding an outlet in rage. "I'd sooner cuddle up to Stromfeld than go near Simon Macey again."

"No, no, Lori," mused Jake. "Let's not be too hasty."

"Too *what*?"

"Macey doesn't know I taped him. We've got the advantage now, and maybe there's some way we can use it." Jake smiled conspiratorially at Lori. "Know what I mean?"

"I'm beginning to." Lori returned Jake's smile.

"Maybe there's some way we can turn the tables on Simon Macey and Solo Team."

The temperature was dropping alarmingly. Clad only in their swimsuits, Cally and Eddie were beginning to shiver uncontrollably. And now it was as though night had fallen, the deepest, darkest night of the year. Paradise was poisoned.

"Correction," said Eddie. "Make that big trouble. Let's leave it for the techs to sort out. Voice ID Nelligan: End program."

"Voice ID Cross: End program."

And that would be it, of course. Ending the program would initiate a safe, swift transfer from the virtual world to the cyber-cradles at Spy High where the students' flesh-and-blood bodies patiently awaited their minds' return, safe from harm. The system was perfect. Nothing could go wrong. Only one second was needed for the transference mechanism to activate.

Wind struck Cally and Eddie head-on, like a battering ram, knocking them backward across the sand. But the wind was not the greatest shock.

"It's not working!" Cally cried. "End program! Voice ID Cross: End program!"

"Try, 'End program, *please*,'" suggested Eddie, scrambling to his feet again. He stared up at the thunder clouds. White lights sparked and crackled like electricity. "I've got a feeling someone doesn't like us."

From above, a lightning bolt daggered directly at them. Astonished by the quickness of his own reflexes, Eddie threw himself and Cally out of its path. The beach combusted where they'd been, atomizing Eddie's abandoned sunglasses.

"Put my mind at ease, Cal," he urged. "Tell me what's happening."

"Something's overridden the program." Eddie didn't like the look in Cally's eyes. "Something hostile. Something that doesn't want us to leave."

"Can I guess yet?"

A second bolt of lightning split the nearest palm tree asunder, sending flames shooting into the air. And the dark clouds above were now spinning and spiraling in a dizzy, whirling pattern as the ground began to shake.

"Nemesis." Cally hissed the name. "It knows we're here. It's coming for me, Eddie." She held on to him tightly.

"Yeah? Well it's not going to get you." He tried to sound confident. The spy with a smile. "Not with Eddie Nelligan at your back, remember? Come on." He dragged her toward the pitiful cover of the palms. "Think, Cal. There's got to be a way out. There's got to be a backup procedure in case of system breakdown, hasn't there?"

"You're right." Cally nodded, trying to think straight. ("Organic . . . forms . . . im . . . pure . . .") Trying to forget that and the strangling hands of zombie scientists wasn't easy. "Maybe the techs back in the chamber . . . they'll know something's wrong . . ." But she'd been stupid, stupid to allow Eddie to persuade her to come here. She should have realized, should have known better. But she'd been tired. She hadn't been thinking. In the virtual world, Nemesis was the hunter. And Cally had just made herself prey.

There was a whirlpool in the sky. At its center, a single, staring eye. A beam like a searchlight stabbed out of it and prowled across the ravaged beach toward the palm trees.

Eddie dragged Cally deeper into the undergrowth. "Listen, we'll be all right," he promised. "We can't be harmed in here anyway, can we? I mean, this is only virtual reality, right? Our physical bodies are perfectly safe. Aren't they?"

The light beam probed through the foliage, closing in on the students inexorably, inevitably. The vortex in the sky seemed to be building to some violent crescendo.

"If only." Eddie stumbled, and Cally almost fell over him. She gripped his shoulders, trying hard to make him understand the peril of their situation. "It's our minds that matter, our minds that are sending signals back to our bodies. And our minds believe this is real."

"So if we believe we're hurt . . ." Eddie's heart chilled with understanding.

"Nemesis will have overridden the safety protocols. If we die here, we'll die for real."

"Im . . . pure . . ."

Both students screamed as pain raked across their minds like claws. The voice of Nemesis was like fingernails scraping on a blackboard, piercing, screeching.

"Organic . . . forms . . . impure . . ."

The words were not spoken aloud. They were in the teenagers' heads, like broken glass in their brains.

And now the light had found them, stripping away their flimsy cover. Cally's skull felt like it was on fire and every limb ached. She couldn't see perfectly what happened next, which was probably just as well.

The sky split open and midnight rain splattered the students like warm blood. The vortex gaped like a rotting mouth. Something forced its way through, something that glittered darkly and pulsated with power.

Cally had glimpsed the face of Nemesis before, its bulging black eyes and the cold, computerized codes behind them, its robotic maw and the electrodes within, its digital glare of hatred. But now its spidery legs, like spiked steel pylons, like gleaming metal girders, prodded from the vortex and sought purchase on the sand of the beach. The jagged, machine body followed, the head, the glinting, calculating eyes, the electrode fangs that sparked with deadly current, and finally the swollen, crackling abdomen, its cybercircuits encased in chitinous armor. The corruption was here. The virus had arrived.

Nemesis towered above the students, fixed them with an implacable stare.

"Organic forms . . . impure . . . eradicate . . ."

"Not what you'd call a conversationalist," muttered Eddie. "Come on, Cal."

If he was looking for an escape route, the options were suddenly reduced. The ground rumbled and then erupted, great pillars of stone hammered up through the soil to hem them in. Nemesis seemed to nod its approval.

"It's remaking the landscape," Cally gasped, "reprogramming in its own image. There's nothing we can do!" Nemesis bore down upon them. "I don't know what to do!"

No jokes now. No time. Eddie placed himself between Cally and Nemesis. "Run! Get as far as you can! I'll hold it off!" He wasn't sure with what. Eddie doubted that courage alone would impress the virus.

With a speed which belied its size, Nemesis's head lunged down and forward, inspecting Eddie like an insect. Instinctively, Eddie threw up his arms to protect himself. The mouth would close on him, and he'd be fried. The current generated by the twin electrodes would cook his internal organs and peel the flesh from his bones like old wallpaper.

He closed his eyes before the end and screamed out, *"No!"*

And there was darkness, true, but no pain. Maybe death had gotten bad press.

Then there were hands on him — human hands — and Eddie realized that he wasn't dead and that was good, and he wasn't in the virtual-reality program anymore, either and that was even better. He was in his cybercradle. The technical assistants were disconnecting him. "Get him free," someone urged, "while we still have control."

"Cally," Eddie demanded. "What about Cally?"

He tried to pull himself out of the cybercradle but was too weak. His head spun and the prospect of being violently sick was imminent. The techs supported him, easing him out. "Steady, Nelligan. Take it slowly. You've survived an ordeal. Just relax."

"Relax?" The word seemed to have no meaning. "Where's Cally? Is she all right?"

The techs exchanged anxious glances. That was a no, then. Eddie snapped his gaze to Cally's cybercradle. It was surrounded by more technical assistants. They were silent, like mourners at a funeral.

"Cally!" Eddie lurched drunkenly toward her cradle. "What's the matter with her? What's going on?" The techs parted and let him through. "Cally? Oh, no . . ."

She might have been sleeping. Her expression was calm, her body at peace, but her mind, that was elsewhere. In a virtual world of its own design, Nemesis evidently still had some use for Cally. She wasn't dead, but she wasn't truly alive, either.

Cally was in a coma.

CHAPTER THIRTEEN

"We can keep her body functioning like this indefinitely," said the tech. "We can feed her nourishment, prevent the muscles from atrophying with physical therapy. She could remain like this for the rest of her natural life."

Sleeping, but not sleeping. Unconscious, but not really that, either. Lacking consciousness, which was different. Lacking a mind. Lacking a soul. The shell of Cally Cross, the memory of her, empty and hollow. Bond Team, the tech, and Senior Tutor Grant were gathered quietly at her cybercradle. *That was wrong now, too,* Lori thought, *the name. A cradle suggested birth, new life.* The receptacle in which Cally's body was stored was more like a coffin now, a coffin with a glass lid, like the one in which the poisoned Snow White lay before she was raised again by the prince. Who was here to be Cally's prince? Who could bring her back to life?

"What about her mind?" Lori asked, praying for a miracle. "How can we restore it?"

The tech shuffled embarrassedly, looking at no one. "I've told you what we can do," he said. "Returning Cally's consciousness to her is the one thing we cannot. From what Eddie has told us, we must assume that somehow her mind, her personality, her essence, if you will, is stranded in the cyberworld and at the mercy of Nemesis."

"Then we've got to get it out." The solution seemed straightforward to Jake. "Or go in after her. We can't just stand around and do nothing."

"Cally's one of us," Ben echoed. "Whatever it takes, we'll do it."

Jennifer and Lori assented. Eddie mumbled and wished he was in the cradle instead of Cally. Was he imagining it, or were the eyes of the others closed against him, their comments somehow directed at him? Like veiled accusations with the subtext: Why had he allowed Cally to be claimed by Nemesis? Why hadn't he made a stand? And the bottom line: Why was he here without her? Bond Team stood or fell together. And while his teammates didn't say any of these things aloud, Eddie knew they were thinking them. His teammates thought he was a failure.

And why not? They were right, weren't they? He'd failed Cally. And he didn't dare tell them what he realized now had happened at the end. With Nemesis poised to strike, Eddie had expected only death. But the virus hadn't killed him. It had simply sent him away, back to the world of flesh and blood and regret. Nemesis had not even deemed him to be worthy of death. Nemesis had dismissed him like he was nothing. *Nothing.* Seemed Nemesis was a good judge of character.

Jennifer made a suggestion, albeit a suicidal one. Her eyes were blazing. "Can't we be sent into the program? We can fight Nemesis and bring Cally back. She's alive in there, isn't she? It's not too late?"

"No, her consciousness is unimpaired," admitted the tech. "If it was damaged to any life-threatening extent, her vital signs would be affected. But as far as being too late, I'm afraid that's more difficult to determine. If Cally's mind is suffering sustained mental trauma, which we have to concede may be the case, then the consequences for her health if . . . *when* her mind is returned to her body, well, they could be considerable."

"What do you mean?" Lori said.

"Brain damage," the tech winced. "Severe brain damage."

"Then what are we waiting for?" Jennifer seemed already to be picking her cybercradle.

Grant raised his hands like he was surrendering, maybe to the inevitable. "Hold on a minute. Jennifer. All of you. Wait."

"For what?" Jake resented. "Nemesis to finish Cally off?"

"For orders. For your senior tutor to decide what to do." Grant pulled rank. "I know you want to help Cally. We all do. But sending anybody into virtual reality at this point, with Nemesis infecting the system, would be effectively to sign their death warrant. Mr. Deveraux has ordered a total shutdown of all computer systems in the school, apart from those that provide the most vital services, such as Cally's life support, for the duration of this crisis. Our first priority must be to strengthen our security programs and to defend the integrity of our so far unviolated systems." Grant regarded his students gravely. "I'm afraid our work here at Deveraux is more important than any single individual. I'm sorry."

"Say it louder, and Cally might hear you," muttered Jake. "Welcome to the expendables."

Ben gripped his shoulder. "You knew the score when we signed up, Daly. We all did. Cally included."

"Yeah? Is that supposed to make me feel better? Thought you'd be a tad more concerned, Stanton. How are we gonna win the Sherlock Shield with five?"

"Hey, this isn't about —"

Grant broke in, stern, commanding. "Bickering has no place on a team. You won't help Cally like that."

Jennifer laughed humorlessly. "According to you, we won't help her at all."

"The thing is," Lori put in, "we know exactly where Nemesis is now. This is our chance to destroy it. That's Spy High work, isn't it? And if we can rescue Cally at the same time . . ."

Grant acknowledged Lori's point. "Good in principle, Lori. But in practice? We don't yet have a way of attacking Nemesis, though our scientists are working on it, obviously. If only Professor Newbolt was able to contribute. Without him, our chances are slim."

Newbolt, Lori thought. *If they only had old Gadge.* Well, and hope fluttered in her heart, perhaps they did.

Eddie remained in the virtual-reality chamber long after the others had departed. They hadn't called for him to follow them. They hadn't registered his absence. And why should they, he thought bitterly, he was nothing.

Cally lay there, a ghost beneath the glass. He gazed at her. She was like a photograph. "There's no one I'd sooner have at my back," she'd said. Maybe she ought to think again. If only she could think at all.

"I'm sorry, Cal." Not very witty. Not very joker-like in the pack.

Eddie saw his face reflected in the cybercradle's shield. The spy with a smile. Not anymore.

What she was going to do: Was it ethical? Was it right? Did the ends justify the means? Lori wasn't sure. All she knew was that one person and one person alone held the possibility of saving Cally. It wasn't her. In a way, it wasn't even Gadge. That one person was Vanessa.

She found Gadge in his lab, fussing over circuit boards and

flashing lights, mumbling advice to nonexistent students. He didn't even notice her come in. *Happy in his own way,* Lori thought, *senility insulating him from pain and hurt and the memories that scar.* And she was here to remind him of all that tragedy. She was here to raise the dead.

"Grandfather," she said. "Grandfather."

Gadge shuddered, looked up. There was a sudden fear in his face, like the discovery of a guilty secret. "Who is it?" he said. "Who's there?"

"You know who I am, Grandfather." She stepped closer toward him, bringing back the past. She smiled.

And old Gadge smiled, too, and relief and delight were mixed together in his smile. It lit up his whole face as he held out his frail arms to embrace her. "Vanessa," he said, in a voice choked with emotion. "My dear."

Lori let him hug her. She heard the old man sob. She knew why. "It's good to see you again, Grandfather," she said.

"Let me look at you, Vanessa." His gnarled and quivering hands roamed over her face, her hair, the way a blind man might identify someone he knows. "Ah, you visit me so rarely these days, my dear. You don't know how much I miss you."

"I do, Grandfather, but you mustn't. There's no need. I'm happy where I am." Lori thought she'd better move matters along quickly. The deception was troubling her more the longer it lasted. *Think of Cally,* she reminded herself. *This is for Cally.*

Gadge seemed to age visibly. "Happy? How can you be, Vanessa? I did something, didn't I? I did something to make you go away, and I was wrong. It was my fault, wasn't it? I can't quite remember what I did but if you stay a while I'm sure I will . . ."

"It doesn't matter, Grandfather," Lori soothed. "Not any-

more. That's what I came to say. It doesn't matter what you did.
I forgive you. I've always loved you, and I forgive you."

"You forgive me, Vanessa?" Old Gadge held back the tears
with difficulty. "Oh, my dear, how I hoped you'd one day tell me
that. I'm sorry for what I did, so terribly sorry. But I thought . . .
I can't remember what I thought . . . but thank you, my dear.
I've always loved you, too." He held her hand and stroked it like
a kitten.

"Grandfather." Now was the moment of truth. "There's something else."

"Anything for you, Vanessa. Anything, my dear girl."

"I need you to help me."

Jennifer opened the door when he knocked, but while Jake
didn't expect her to fling her arms around him, certainly not
given the present circumstances, he didn't expect the coldness
and the sternness in her expression, either. It was as if the more
important door, the one that provided access to Jennifer's heart
and soul, was not only closed but had been fitted with new
chains.

"Lori's not here," Jennifer said, and smiled thinly like she'd
made a joke.

"What?"

"You can come in and have a look if you don't believe me.
Bathroom, wherever. She's not even under the bed."

"What?" Jake wondered about going out and coming in
again. "I'm not looking for Lori, Jen. I don't understand why . . ."
He never thought of Simon Macey. "I came to see you."

"So you've seen me. I hope it's made you happy." She gave
him a quick twirl.

"Are you all right?" He was thinking about what Ben had called her: *unstable.* "I thought maybe we could talk. You know, maybe it'd help us if we talked."

"Talked about what? The nice weather we're having this time of year? Who you might happen to meet on the grounds when taking a walk?"

"About Cally, actually."

"Oh, Cally. She's in a coma, didn't you know that? Still, that means we can do things behind her back, and she won't be any the wiser. Kind of useful when you think about it, isn't it?"

"Listen, I know we're all upset, but . . ." Jake didn't know quite how to take Jennifer's behavior. He was beginning to wish Lori was there. Or, indeed, anyone. "And I thought we could talk about us maybe."

"*Us?*" Jennifer seemed incredulous. "Us as in you and me? Just the two of us?"

"Well, the other day, in the dome, in the field, I thought maybe something was happening. You know, between us. I thought we were beginning to feel . . ."

"What?" Why was he saying this after she'd seen him with Lori?

"Listen, Jen, why don't we sit down and talk?"

"I don't think so." He'd betrayed her. She couldn't rely on him. She couldn't rely on anyone. "I'm otherwise occupied. But I'm sure you'll find someone who's interested. If you know what I mean."

Jake didn't, but he left anyway. He couldn't deal with Jennifer in this mood. If she wanted to be alone, then she was going the right way about it.

He headed back to his own room. Maybe someone had

come up with a plan for helping Cally. Anything would do, however unlikely or outrageous, just so long as it was action. He'd never felt comfortable talking. Fighting, though, that was another matter.

Lori found Ben in the virtual-reality chamber. He was with Cally, head bowed, deep in thought. His hand rested on the cybercradle. He only realized Lori was there when her hand joined his and squeezed reassuringly.

"You've got to watch that," Lori chided gently. "Not good for a secret agent to get crept up on so easily."

Ben smiled weakly. "I wish I could say I knew it was you, Lo. Maybe I'm losing my touch."

"No," comforted Lori. "What's happened to Cally is just affecting us all. But listen, Ben —"

"Do you think I'm a good leader?"

She was startled by the question but could tell from Ben's frank expression that he was serious.

"It's something Jake said. He made out that the only reason I was concerned about Cally was because of the impact her loss might have on the team. Like I didn't really care about her at all."

"Jake didn't mean it," Lori said. "He was lashing out without thinking, that's all. We all say things that we don't really mean when we're stressed out."

"You don't, Lo," Ben said. "You never lose your temper. You're never sarcastic. You never do things behind people's backs."

"Come on," Lori colored and shook her head. "Don't believe it. I'm not a saint."

"You're an Angel," Ben smiled. "But me, I sometimes think I'm down there in the other place with the guys with the horns and the forked tails. Because whatever you say, and however right you might be about Jake and what he said, I'm afraid part of it might be true."

"Ben, you're tormenting yourself for no reason."

"No, I've got a reason. It's called selfishness. It's called arrogance. It's called wanting to be the best at any cost. And sometimes it makes me act in ways that a good leader shouldn't act, and sometimes, it makes me treat people, I don't know, like they're less than me."

"You're strong. You push us. You make Bond Team what we are."

"Did I make Cally what she is now?"

"Of course not." Lori shook him, angered now. "Nobody's to blame for Cally. None of us. You were right what you said before. We all knew the risks. If we can't take them, then we can be mind-wiped and sent home. Blaming ourselves for something that's not our fault is just self-pity and self-indulgence. That's the sign of a bad leader. A good leader accepts what's done and tries to put it right."

Ben indicated Cally's cybercradle. "So how do we put this right?"

Lori gripped his hand more tightly. "That's what I wanted to tell you."

There were others in the lab, too, the rest of Bond Team, and Grant, even Deveraux via a videoscreen link, but Professor Henry Newbolt seemed to be largley unaware of them. Gadge only had eyes for Lori, and they were eyes that once again blazed with genius and originality. For the moment, at least, the inventor was back.

"This is how we'll do it, my dear," he explained. "This is how we'll save your friend."

Eddie expected Gadge to produce a variation on a ray gun or something, a weapon that would blast Nemesis into a million spidery pieces. Instead, the scientist produced a garment in shimmering silver material, not unlike a one-piece shock suit. It reminded him of the old radiation suits they'd used to wear at atomic plants, not one inch of skin exposed, a filmy visor shielding the face. The old Eddie, the spy with a smile, would have made a quip about the lack of fashion sense being enough to frighten Nemesis away, or that he hadn't realized that Gucci was outfitting Spy High students now, or something equally inane. The new Eddie, the Eddie who was nothing, watched closely and listened attentively. If there was a second chance coming, he wasn't going to miss it.

"You need to go back into the program," Gadge continued. "That's the only way. But you need to make yourselves immune to the power of the virus. Hence the ViPr: the Virus Protection suit. Set a snake to snare a spider, Vanessa."

"Vanessa?" Everybody but Ben turned to Lori quizzically.

Lori ignored them all. "Go on, Grandfather." More general bemusement. "What exactly does the suit do?"

"When activated," Gadge supplied, "the ViPr generates a force field that acts as a counteragent to the virus's ability to influence and reprogram cyberspace. In other words, with your suits switched on, Nemesis won't be able to harm you. You'll wear these in your cybercradles to protect your bodies while virtual versions will be configured into the software, so that you'll also be safe in the program itself."

"Sounds good," Jake approved.

"If it works," Jennifer sulked.

"Oh, it'll work." Gadge seemed inordinately positive. "I wouldn't create anything for my Vanessa that didn't . . . work . . ." Suddenly a shadow crossed his smile.

Lori interpreted it as bad news. "How, Grandfather?" Keep his mind off the past. Make Gadge believe in the present. "How does it work?"

"Oh, in simple terms," the old man rallied, "the ViPr resembles the way the human immune system produces antibodies to fight infection, only instead of antibodies, the suit generates antibinaries, computer code that defends against even superviruses such as Nemesis. And better yet, the antibinaries can attack as well as defend." Gadge drew his audience's attention to the wristbands woven into the suit. "Functions just like sleepshot, only firing antibinaries. And for when you've saved . . ." Again, that moment of doubt, of forgetfulness, lucidity, ebbing away. "When . . . you've saved . . . Vanessa?"

"It's all right, Grandfather." Lori sensed that she was losing him. The old man's mind was slipping. "Tell me, what's that? What have you got there?"

Gadge regarded the laptop-sized metal device on the table as if he'd never seen it before. "What . . . here? A bomb!" It was as if he'd remembered the final answer in a quiz. "A binary . . . bomb. Set it up . . . set it off. . . . Antibinaries will flood the program . . . break it down entirely. No escape for Nemesis, for anybody caught in the program then. You have to be back before detonation or . . . you can't be saved. No, you can't." An awful truth at last overwhelmed him. "Vanessa, I didn't save you . . ." He gazed in tragic horror at Lori. "I never saved . . ." And then the old eyes glazed, as if the life had left them. "You're not Vanessa. Who are you? Who are you people? What are you doing in my lab? Can't a man get on with his work without interruption? Leave me alone. Go away, and leave me alone. . . ." The broken old man who'd once been among the most brilliant minds in the world scuttled away, into a corner, muttering, and busied himself with loose strands of wire.

"So are you going to explain what just happened there, Lori?" Jake inquired.

Lori looked after Gadge with pity. "Something I'm not particularly proud of."

"But very resourceful of you, Angel." Deveraux's voice over the videoscreen surprised them. "Using Professor Newbolt's memories of his granddaughter to effect even a temporary mental recovery. By so doing, you have given us a chance — both to save Cross and destroy Nemesis once and for all."

"But the suits, sir," Grant cautioned, "they're untested."

"We don't have time to test them, Grant," Deveraux said. "Time is our enemy. We have to act now, before Nemesis moves on, and we lose it. Assemble a team at the virtual-reality chamber."

"Sir!" Ben stepped forward. "Send us, sir. We know Nemesis better than anyone here, and Cally's one of us. We owe it to her."

Deveraux's finely chiseled features considered the request. "Grant?"

"Stanton has a point, sir, but there are graduate teams —"

"As students, we cannot require you to undertake this mission," Deveraux pointed out, "but if it is your wish as a team to volunteer, then you will be assigned. It is your choice, Bond Team. Does Stanton speak for you all?"

* * *

Apparently, he did. Ben eased into his cybercradle as the techs busily prepared the chamber for transfer. Nobody had objected to the mission; everyone had supported him. It had made him feel good, like a leader again, and that was enough. Whatever dangers awaited them when they confronted Nemesis this final time, Ben knew that he and his teammates would face and overcome them. They were Bond Team. They didn't know how to lose.

"We'll send in a ViPr suit for Cally with you, and the binary bomb. Prime it before you do anything else. Destroying Nemesis is your overriding priority."

Lori knew it. She'd deluded Professor Newbolt for this, for the chance to strike back, to stop the virus before it could kill anyone else. Before it could kill Cally. As she strapped herself into her cybercradle, Lori hoped that poor, dead Vanessa would have understood. And she prayed that they weren't already too late.

"We're going to be redirecting energy from our security program to the VR systems to ensure that we can transfer you back, but we can't keep that up forever. You'll have one hour. You'll need to locate and rescue Cally within sixty minutes."

Time limits never bothered Jake. They provided a challenge, not an obstacle. He relaxed his muscles and breathed deeply, as they'd been taught to do before a total virtual-reality transfer. He didn't think of Jennifer (although part of him wanted to). He thought of Cally. Last term, he'd persuaded her to stay at Spy High. He hadn't done that to see her turned into a vegetable. So they had one hour to put things right. Jake intended to make it count.

"Nemesis has the advantage. It will have been able to rework the program into whatever kind of environment it likes by now. There's no way of knowing what you'll face."

Jennifer didn't care. *The darker, the deadlier, the more horrific the scenario the better,* she thought. It would match her mood. The virtual sensors pressed against her temples. She felt the cybercradle cramping her, restricting her. She wanted to scream. She wanted to lash out. Soon now. Very soon.

With the slightest of hisses the glass shields of the cybercradles descended, clicked into place. "Good luck, Bond Team," someone said. The transference began.

Eddie closed his eyes. No more jokes now about two in a cybercradle. Or if they're cradles, why don't they rock? Or what happened to the lullabies? Or anything like that. The others hadn't encountered Nemesis in the cyberflesh before. He had, and then he'd been found wanting, but not this time. *This time,* Eddie vowed, *it was going to be different.*

CHAPTER FOURTEEN

"This is not good," said Ben.

It was postapocalyptic. All around them were the smoking skeletons of a ruined city: ruptured roads, the shells of cars, walls jagged against the sky like giant and broken teeth, the bones of buildings rotting in a radioactive wasteland. Above them, clouds were blocking out the pitiful sun. Clouds that were seething and suppurating like evil itself, stabbing themselves with scarlet lightning.

"Mankind's final nightmare," breathed Lori. "Nuclear Armageddon."

"Yeah." Jake's expression was grim behind his visor. "And Nemesis's ultimate dream. This is what it wants to see in the real world."

"Not if we can help it." Ben adjusted his suit. "Check your ViPr suits. Make sure they're fully activated. Helmet communicators all right? Can everybody hear me?"

"Loud and clear, leader man," said Eddie.

"Good. 'Cause if your suit fails, Nemesis has got you."

Jennifer stood a little distance away from the others. She found the devastated landscape both disturbing and strangely stimulating. "Well, are we doing anything or what?" she demanded restlessly. "An hour doesn't last forever."

"We've got to wait, Jen," Ben reminded her. "For Cally's suit and the bomb."

Alongside Eddie, the ground rippled, as though it had suddenly become liquid. Solid objects materialized. "Speedy delivery," Eddie said.

"Okay." Ben knelt by the bomb. "Lori, stay with me and make sure I'm doing this right. The rest of you, quick reconnaissance. Any sign of Cally or Nemesis — any sign of anything — and I want to know about it."

Ben focused on setting up the bomb. Lori took charge of Cally's bundled suit and watched him proudly. This was the Ben she loved. Decisive. Inspiring. A leader. How could she have been tempted by the sham that was Simon Macey? If they ever got out of here alive, she'd make it up to Ben, she promised.

"So where's the big bad spider, then?" Jennifer wondered, with more than a hint of a sneer.

Eddie and Jake joined her. "Don't worry," Eddie said. "If it's anywhere near, you'll see it. But let me tell you, the longer we can stay out of Nemesis's way, the better."

"It must know we're here by now," Jake reasoned. "Why doesn't it attack?"

"Maybe it doesn't think we're a threat," Eddie ventured, wondering if more than maybe he was right.

"Jake, Eddie . . ." The sneer had gone from Jennifer's voice. "What's that?"

Something in the distance, but moving in their direction. Trickling across the cracked and pitted landscape like a thick layer of tar, black and bubbling. A dark tide that washed over everything in its path.

Within minutes, everything in its path would include Bond Team.

"Ben!" Jake called. "Better make it quick with that bomb. We might be needing it sooner than we thought."

"All right, we're done," Ben announced with triumph. "So what's up?" He and Lori dashed to their teammates' side.

But the black river was not a single substance after all. They could see that now. It was not a liquid but a swarm of small creatures, glittering like lumps of coal. Like insects. Spiders. Thousands upon thousands of cyberspiders scuttling toward them with hostile intent. Nemesis had some new friends.

"It's been breeding. Reproducing itself somehow," deduced Lori in horror.

"Let's hope Cally's off in the other direction," Eddie gulped. "'Cause I think that's where we should be heading."

They turned.

They were surrounded.

"Well, here's where we check out the suits," Ben gritted. "Form a circle. Make a stand. Fry these suckers."

They didn't need to aim. Their wristguns blasted the advancing army with antibinary particles exactly as Gadge had described, scorching swathes of fire through their numbers. The cyberbodies crisped and curled like old leaves in a bonfire. The burning stench rose to further pollute the air.

"Yeah!" Eddie was first to use both wrist weapons at the same time, zigzagging blazing mayhem with abandon. "Yeah!" He was beginning to feel a lot better.

Jennifer, too, was finding release in the slaughter, but Ben was controlling his own urge to indulge in emotional outbursts. A leader had to keep cool even in times of stress. A leader had to consider and assess all conceivable possibilities. And one rather disturbing possibility had just occurred to him.

What if their wristguns ran out of power? What if the supply of antibinaries dried up? And what if Nemesis's brood kept on coming?

They were already only yards away.

"Conserve your power!" Ben yelled. "We don't know how long the suits can last. Fire one weapon only!"

"You're the boss," responded Eddie, "but I'm thinking we need more firepower, not less."

A ring of flame protected Bond Team, sintering the cyber-spiders that surged blindly into it. There were so many of them. Like lemmings, they came on. And suddenly some of them broke through, and they were launching themselves at the teenagers' bodies. Jake cried out as several of the things landed on his chest. He jerked instinctively to swipe them away. Didn't need to. The suit, crackling with antibinaries itself, turned the creatures into flares. They shriveled. They died. But they always had replacements.

They leaped at Lori's visor, attacking the eyes. She saw their quivering forms for the slightest of seconds before her sight was blinded by their bursting into flames. And then, shockingly, heart-stoppingly, they weren't bursting into anything. They weren't even getting sunburned. They were clinging on, clogging her vision. She swept at them with her hand and realized with even greater terror that her wristgun was also less effective now, draining in power. "Ben!" They were crawling all over her. "My suit!" Her visor was blackened with the things. Soon they'd be gnawing their way through the flimsy material, their fangs at her face. "Ben!" Lori screamed.

Then they were gone. Ben was holding her, and the others were close, too. And the cyberspiders were in retreat, leaving behind them only the charred remains of their brethren.

Eddie gasped, nearly doubling over with relief and exhaustion. "So is that a win for us or what?"

"Why did they leave?" Lori wanted to know. "They could have had us. My suit was losing power by the second. Much longer and . . ." She shuddered.

"Don't worry, Lo. The suit will recharge itself," Ben said. *I hope*, he thought.

"But Lori's right," mused Jake. "We were on the point of being overwhelmed. I don't understand why . . ."

"So Nemesis isn't a master tactician," contributed Jennifer. "Or it wasn't aware that we were on our last legs. Or maybe that was just the first assault."

"I think I prefer options one and two," Eddie said.

"If only." Jake's eyes narrowed. He sensed further danger. The ground under their feet rumbled. It sounded like a subway train, but it wasn't.

Bond Team was scattered like bowling pins as the street erupted, and Nemesis itself rose up among them.

They were fighting for their lives, Senior Tutor Elmore Grant knew. They were battling to save their friend, perhaps to save countless others whom they'd never even met from the madness of Nemesis. And yet you wouldn't know it, not as their bodies slumbered peacefully in the cybercradles, bodies that Grant would be sending home in boxes if the mission went wrong. And it could go wrong, just as easily as it could go right. A Spy High training was no guarantee of survival.

Some agents lived, Grant reasoned. Some agents died. And some former agents were forced to endure an existence somewhere between the two. Like himself. The top half of him was living, was flesh and blood and bone, but his legs were synthetic, had been since his final mission in the field and the explosion that had ended his career. In reality, Senior Tutor Elmore Grant was only half a man.

He ran his hands through his hair. So he had to wait. He had to stay here in the virtual-reality chamber and guess at the dangers his students were facing. He could pray for them, but he couldn't aid them. He was helpless. And it was a terrible thing for a man like himself to be helpless, to be a bystander. But that was all he was. That was what he'd been reduced to. He had to wait.

They were fighting for their lives, Senior Tutor Elmore Grant knew. How he envied them.

They froze and stared. It was understandable. The sudden appearance of a twelve-foot-high sentient computer virus in the approximate form of a spider would probably have been sufficient to leave anybody frozen and staring. Unfortunately, the members of Bond Team were not supposed to be just anybody. They were supposed to have been trained to expect the unexpected, to let nothing faze them or delay their purpose. Because for Bond Team, delay could mean death. And it could be instant.

Lori only had time for an impression of Nemesis's massiveness, the crackling of dark energies at its eyes, its abdomen, and along the razor edges of its eight black legs. Its head swiveled, calculating its enemies' strength. She didn't have time for evasive action. She didn't have time to move at all.

Nemesis lashed at her with one of its legs. The limb caught her and lifted her into the air. She crashed to the fractured street and expected death. The cyberflesh had glittered like a blade. She should have been sliced open. But she wasn't. Her suit had not been compromised. She was alive.

And if she was alive, she could fight.

Lori scrambled to her feet. The others were already firing their wristguns at Nemesis, though still beating a strategic retreat toward her. Flames ignited against the virus's steel sides, but none were slowing it down, none were taking hold. Lori sensed renewed power in her suit. Ben had been right. The antibinaries had recharged themselves. Now it was her turn.

Lori aimed her anger at Nemesis. She fired. Flames exploded at its abdomen.

"Good shooting, Lo!" shouted Ben. "Are you all right?"

"I'd be better if we could stop this thing in its tracks."

"We're hurting it!" Jake claimed, and the screeches issuing from Nemesis certainly supported his contention. "But not enough. We're right in the source of its power here. We're just not packing enough punch."

"What will it take for this monster to fall?" Jennifer cried.

Then she was ducking, rolling out of the way as the spider's front legs scythed once more through the poisoned air. Bond Team scattered, regrouped, and fired again.

It was a pattern they could probably maintain throughout the remaining minutes of the hour. Which meant it wasn't going to get them anywhere, Ben reasoned. An endless standoff with Nemesis was not going to locate Cally. They — he — needed to be more proactive.

He hoped to God the ViPr suits were everything Gadge had said they would be.

"Ben!" Lori screamed. "Wait!" Why was he running directly toward the virus?

"Come on, you ugly sucker! Come and get me! Show me what you've got!" *And then I'll show you what I've got,* Ben promised.

"He's lost it!" Eddie was flabbergasted. "He's lost his mind!"

"Then let's go after him. Why are we even talking about it?" Jennifer continued her attack.

"No, wait, Jen!" Jake restrained her. "Ben knows what he's doing."

But even Nemesis seemed shocked that one of the intruders should offer himself up to his inevitable fate so generously. The organic form was standing within striking distance of its elec-trodes, shouting defiance and shaking its fists but not even firing the weapons that stung. Such reckless behavior did not com pute with the data that Nemesis had gathered on the human species. Such futile demonstrations of bravado were not logical. They deserved to be punished.

Nemesis's head dropped like a guillotine. It swallowed Ben to the waist.

Everyone but Jake cried out in horror. "Get ready!" Jake urged.

And then Nemesis's head exploded.

Sections of skull, brain, and eyeball sprayed across the street, fizzling like shorted circuits. What was left of the cyber-spider's mouth retreated twitching from Ben, who fired his wristguns again, disintegrating the head further. His suit was slick with an oil-like blood, but he was unharmed.

"Finish it off!" Jake ordered. "Now!"

The rest of Bond Team charged at the tottering Nemesis, firing furiously. The virus seemed unable to sustain its chosen form now. The brittle legs snapped. The armored abdomen ruptured, and liquid spilled out. The cleansing fires of the anti-binary particles went to work on the creature's grotesque body.

And Nemesis fell in flames to the ground.

"We've done it!" yelled Jennifer. "We killed you. We *killed* you!"

Lori rushed to Ben's side. He was wobbling. She caught him and eased him down onto one knee. "Ben," and she wanted to kiss him, but a pair of visors between them was a minor problem. "What on earth? You could have been killed. What did you think you were doing?"

"That was disgusting," said Eddie, with an expression to match.

"It was the bravest thing I've ever seen." Lori glared at him.

"Yeah, well," Eddie adapted, "that's what I meant, Lo. The bravest, most disgusting thing I've ever seen." And in his head, he was thinking, *That's why Ben is leader, and I'm just the nobody who makes smart remarks.* And in his head, he was asking, *Could I do that? Could I risk sacrificing myself for the others, for the team? And if not, why am I even here? When will my chance come?*

"Now that's what I call *point-blank range.*" Jake nodded his admiration. "Nice work, Ben."

"Thanks. Yeah." Ben's suit was gradually sizzling away all traces of Nemesis's innards. He was pleased about that and even more about his plan's success. "I thought that the only way we might be able to overcome Nemesis was if we could get close enough to blast through its defenses."

"Yeah, and you can't get much closer than inside the thing's mouth," Jake chuckled. "You've always been a tough act to swallow, Ben."

"Well, just don't ask me for a repeat performance," Ben said.

"Nobody's going to need to," said Lori.

"Uh, guys." It was Jennifer. She sounded anxious. "I wouldn't bet on that if I were you. Something's happening. Something not good."

Nemesis lived. At least, its constituent parts still seemed to be alive. How else could their independent movement be explained, the disturbing ability of loose scraps of casing to inch toward one another and fuse themselves together, circuit seeking circuit, shards of limbs combining and extending?

"It's reconstructing itself," Jennifer observed with awe. "It's a cyberresurrection."

"So let's kill it again before it screws its head back on." Eddie looked like he wanted to lead the way.

Ben struggled to his feet, leaning on Lori. He shook his head despondently. "It's no good, Eddie. It didn't work, after all. We can't kill it, whatever we do, not completely, not with anything less than the bomb."

"So what do we do, Ben?" Jennifer watched as legs snapped together like poles, as the creature's abdomen inflated like a balloon. "It's getting the hang of this."

"We've got no choice," Ben decided. "We leave Nemesis to the bomb. We can't kill it but it can't kill us either, not in the ViPr suits. So we find Cally. Right now."

They moved off quickly across the decimated landscape, although Jennifer couldn't resist a final, parting gesture. A clump of eyeball squirmed its way past her foot to join the rest of

Nemesis's head. One brief blast of her wristgun, and it was bon-fired. "Fix that," she muttered.

They spread out in a line to cover the maximum ground possi-ble, picking their way across the crumbling city and keeping in constant touch with one another through their helmet commu-nicators. On missions, it was good to talk, even if most of the time it had to be in whispers or monosyllables, or both.

"Watch where you step," hissed Ben, proving the point. "Lots of holes and stuff. You fall down in one of those, and it's bad news. Your suits can't mend a broken leg."

Eddie wondered whether that meant that if any of them did suffer an accident here among the ruins, Ben would lead their teammates on regardless. He doubted it, but he was feeling pretty left behind as it was, relegated to the far end of the line. He shouldn't take it personally, he knew. After all, there was an-other end of the line with Jennifer on it, but somehow he just felt distanced from the heart of things. Maybe if he could spot Cally, then everything would be all right.

But even that privilege was denied him.

"Ben! All of you!" Jennifer was not whispering now. "Over here! Over here!"

Of course, it would be that Eddie had the farthest to go.

"What is it, Jen?" Ben voiced. "Is it Cally?"

Dismay, almost palpable, even over the communicator. "I think so."

She thinks so? Eddie scrambled desperately over the stone ribs of dead buildings. She thought so? What could Jennifer see? What horrors had he abandoned Cally to?

He heard his teammates, one by one, as they reached Jennifer's position. "Oh, my God . . . I don't believe it . . . Ben . . ."

They were just up ahead now, crouched low, and peering over a ridge of rubble. At Cally? He raced to their side. "What is it? What is it?"

"Eddie, keep down!" Ben ordered.

Eddie dropped to the ground. He saw Ben and Jake ashen faced, the girls horrified, disgusted. He lifted his head to see what they had seen.

And then he knew why.

CHAPTER FIFTEEN

In what once had been a doorway, in what once had been a wall, Cally was hanging. One arm was above her, almost as if it were waving, while the other was dangling at her side. Her legs were crooked, like a broken doll's, and neither reached the ground. They didn't have to. Cally was held in place by a web that had been strung between the doorposts, a web in which she was hopelessly enmeshed, a web that might have been the work of a spider if it weren't for the current that seemed to hum through it and that made its strands function more like electrical wires or cables.

Worse, the ground below Cally was thick with cyberspiders, swarming at the base of the web, crawling over the shattered bricks — even daring to climb Cally's unflinching legs, speckling her skin like the march of some foul disease.

And worse still, Nemesis itself, towered above Cally. Unmarked. Unwounded. Reborn. The calculations behind its rows of restored eyes seemed to say one thing: bait.

But worst of all was Cally's possible condition. Her head was hung drunkenly to one side.

"She's not moving," Lori said what the others were thinking. "Ben, what if we're too late? What if Cally's . . . you know . . ."

"We're not. She's not." Ben defied reality to disagree. "She's just unconscious. We just have to get her off that web, get the suit on her, and all go home. Then this place gets blown to pieces."

"And soon," Jennifer reminded him. "So how do we get rid of Nemesis?"

Ben considered quickly. "We need a diversion. If we split into two groups, me and Lori, you, Jen, Jake and . . . Eddie?"

There was no sign of him.

"Where'd he go?"

"I didn't notice. He was just here. . . ."

"If he's playing some kind of stupid game . . ." warned Ben.

"I don't think so," judged Jake. "I think you've got yourself your diversion. Look."

This was his chance. As soon as he saw Cally caught in Nemesis's webbing, those loathsome bugs all over her, he knew it. This was the moment for Eddie Nelligan to prove himself, to redeem himself. And he wasn't going to blow it.

He slipped away with frightening ease while the others were staring at Cally and Nemesis. He could be decisive when he wanted to be. He was thinking *diversion* before Ben had even mentioned the word, and it seemed clear to him that his idea was the only kind of diversion that could work. Eddie circled away from the others. It wasn't going to be good enough for him or anyone else simply to distract Nemesis's attention. The virus knew that in their ViPi suits they couldn't be hurt. If the suit was deactivated, however, Nemesis might be persuaded to abandon Cally.

Eddie broke cover, edged out into the decimated area where Cally was being held. It might have been the uneven surface of the debris that was making his legs shake or it might not. Any moment now and Nemesis could be on him.

"Eddie, what do you think you're doing? Get down, Eddie. It'll see you . . . Can you hear me, Eddie? Take cover. That's an order . . ."

But now was not the time for Eddie to listen to orders. "Calm down, Ben," he said, far from calm himself, "or you'll give yourself a coronary. I'm going to lead Nemesis away, and when I do, go in for Cal. See you later." The eternal optimist. The spy with a smile.

"Eddie, this is not . . ."

He deactivated his communicator. Then he deactivated his suit.

Nemesis sensed him immediately. It raised its head like an animal suddenly aware of a new smell. Something had changed in the virtual world, and it seemed to be to the virus's advantage.

Eddie gave it some help. "Hey, ugly, I'm from Rent-a-Victim. Seems you've been in touch with an . . ." He didn't finish the sentence. The force of Nemesis's hate slammed into him like a Light Train at full speed. Eddie fell to his knees, clasping his ears, not even able to hear himself screaming. No protection. No active antibinaries to insulate him from the psychic assault.

Through vision blistered with pain, he saw the virus stalking toward him. If he didn't get up, if he didn't get moving, that Rent-a-Victim quip could be his epitaph.

Eddie staggered to his feet, turned and ran, wishing he had a SkyBike handy. He didn't look behind. It wouldn't be encouraging to watch Nemesis gaining on him like an eight-legged angel of death. Besides, he had to concentrate on the terrain, the treacherously loose piles of rubble, the sudden gaping pits and slants of fallen wall. If he fell, there'd be no getting up again.

He hoped the others would be with Cally now. He'd given them their opening.

Eddie darted through a doorway where Nemesis could not follow, and the building's surviving wall was big. The virus would have to go around it. That would slow it down.

Only it didn't. Nemesis smashed through the wall and kept on coming.

Maybe this hadn't been such a good idea, after all. But surely, he'd lured the creature far enough away? Surely, he could afford to reactivate his suit?

The ground collapsed in front of him. Eddie cried out, tipped forward, felt the world caving in, a ringing in his ears, and the sickening thud of impact.

Eddie groaned. He'd plunged into some sort of cellar and landed on his back. He tried to move. His legs were trapped beneath a slab of concrete. At least they didn't feel broken. And at least his arms were free. All he had to do was reactivate his suit, and either wait for the others or wait for the transfer. It could only be minutes now.

All he had to do was reactivate his suit . . .

All he had to do was . . .

All . . . over.

The suit must have been damaged in the fall. Nothing was happening.

"Eddie, this is not the way. Get back . . . he's turned off his communicator." Ben gaped at the others, as if Eddie's temerity at cutting him off in mid-command was the most shocking thing of all.

"Nemesis has seen him," Jennifer observed. "It's after him!"

"He's either more stupid or more courageous than we've ever given him credit for," said Jake.

"We've got to help him!" declared Lori, already on her feet.

Ben caught hold of her arm, gently but firmly. "No. Eddie's made his choice. Our priority is Cally. Let's get down there before Nemesis calls off the chase."

There was no advantage in concealing themselves further. With a loud battle cry, the remaining four members of Bond Team launched themselves from the ridge and hurtled toward the captive form of Cally. Their wristguns blazed. Half of the cyberspiders had ignited before their computer brains even registered the attack. The others scurried to meet the enemy.

"Protect Lori!" Ben ordered. "She's got Cally's suit. Keep her between us!"

He took the lead himself, Lori dropping behind him, with Jennifer and Jake on the flanks. Well-aimed antibinaries scorched a clear path to the doorway. Cyberspiders threw themselves from atop of the wall; Bond Team's accuracy turned them into tiny fireballs.

Ben sliced through the webbing. Lori caught Cally as she fell, lowered her down as gently as possible to the ground. She knelt by her friend's side, anxiously smoothing the hair away from her face, calling her name, and praying she was alive. But Cally remained unconscious. It didn't look good.

"How is she, Lori?" Ben and the others encircled them, keeping the diminishing number of cyberspiders at bay.

"I don't know. I don't know." Lori rubbed Cally's limp hands and cradled her close. "Cally, can you hear me? Cally? I can't get a response, Ben. I don't know what to do!"

"Get the suit on her," prompted Jake.

Awkwardly, clumsily, Lori unrolled Cally's ViPr suit and thrust her limbs into it. It was like dressing an unwieldy and oversized baby. "Come on. Cally," she murmured. "Come on. Come on. Speak to me. Say something." But even with the suit on, there was silence. "Jake, it isn't . . ."

And then a cough, a splutter, a fragile twitch of the head and flutter of the eyelids.

"Cally! Guys, she's alive!" Lori hugged her friend ardently. "Cally, you're all right. It's going to be all right."

"Looking that way," Jake said. He ceased firing. Ben and Jennifer followed suit. The ground around them was black with charred and smoking bodies. There were no cyberspiders left to trouble them.

"Yeah, well let's not start counting chickens," Ben cautioned, "or even spiders. Not until we've put all of cyberspace between us and Nemesis." He consulted the chronometer in his ViPr suit. "And that should be in about three minutes."

Jake grinned. "Which just gives us time to welcome Sleeping Beauty here back into the land of the living. Hey, Cal, how are you?"

She was weak and disorientated, but nothing worse than that, it seemed. The medics would be able to check her out properly when they got back, Ben knew. He didn't kneel alongside her with the others. Instead, he turned away and gazed out across the ravaged city. Ben doubted it was appropriate for a leader to show emotion.

"What's . . . happened?" Cally gripped Lori's hand in alarm. "Where are we?"

"It doesn't matter. Just relax, Cal," Lori counseled. "Everything's fine."

But Cally didn't seem convinced. Her eyes flitted between her teammates. "Eddie," she said. "I remember . . . Eddie was here. Where is he? Where's Eddie?"

Bond Team glanced at each other guiltily. It was a good question.

Maybe he'd be all right anyway. Maybe Nemesis would lose track and just pass him by. Maybe he wouldn't need to do anything but lie quietly where he was and bide his time until the transfer sequence. . . .

Yeah, and maybe there were pigs up there in the torn and tumultuous sky.

Eddie shoved again at the concrete slab on his legs. Arnold Schwarzenegger III probably bench-pressed weights like this before breakfast without even raising a sweat, but working out had never worked out for Eddie Nelligan. And it was too late to start now.

If Nemesis appeared before the transfer, he was dead meat.

But strangely, somehow, Eddie didn't feel like screaming or bursting into tears or breaking into prayer. If anything, he felt satisfied, contented. He had proven himself at last, to the others and to himself. They'd have rescued Cally by now. He trusted them to have done that. His sacrifice, if sacrifice it was doomed to be, was not going to be in vain.

And maybe he'd be all right anyway.

Only he wouldn't. A shadow closed over the cellar, like an eclipse. A black shape loomed. Nemesis peered down at him, and its evil glee raked at Eddie's mind, like talons. He wouldn't cry out. He wouldn't give Nemesis the pleasure.

How long before the transfer? Seconds, surely. If he could just delay the virus, play for time.

"Wait! Don't! Listen to me! I can help you!"

Nemesis wasn't falling for it. A leg like a titanic javelin quivered in midair, selecting its spot with sadistic precision.

Last time, Eddie had been dismissed as a worthless irritation. This time, no such luck.

When it jabbed down, the creature's leg would pierce him just above the navel and plunge right through his body to burst out of his back. He'd be wriggling like an insect on a pin.

Transfer. *Transfer!*

Eddie couldn't help it. He had to scream.

He felt a tingling in his bones.

Certain death speared toward him.

Someone up there loved Eddie Nelligan. Must have. Because instead of Nemesis running him through in one fatal motion, helpful pairs of human hands were on him and hauling him hastily from the cybercradle. His scream reinterpreted itself as a hoot of laughter. The transfer had performed the just-in-the-nick-of-time routine. He was back in the virtual-reality chamber. Spy with a smile? He was a spy in one piece, and that was good enough.

But what about the others? What about Cally?

"Eddie! You're all right!" Lori was already approaching him, attended by her own cluster of concerned techs. She seemed glad to see him. Genuinely. Proved it by flinging her arms around him and hugging him tightly. If he'd gotten his visor up faster, he might have got a kiss as well. "We were so worried. You were so brave."

"Yeah, well, some of us are just gifted that way," Eddie said modestly. "But was it worth it?" He noticed medics rushing into the chamber, bringing with them oxygen and a stretcher. "Cally?"

"She's weak but she's going to be fine," said Lori. "Come on."

She did look weak as the medics lifted her out of her cyber-cradle and onto the stretcher. Ben, Jake, and Jennifer looked on anxiously. "Way to go, Ed," said Jake, but still only managing half a smile.

"Eddie?" Cally seemed dazed, scarcely conscious. "Eddie." She reached out her hand toward him. Eddie took it and squeezed reassuringly. "Thank you for coming back."

"Well, I couldn't just leave you there." Eddie grinned. "You owe me a smoothie, Cal."

Cally smiled drowsily. "I owe you more than that."

"Okay, enough for now," said one of the medics. "We need to get her checked out in the infirmary. Are we ready?"

Cally was wheeled away. She already seemed to be asleep. But that was all right: Sleep was a restorative. And sleep was not coma.

"Eddie." Ben gripped his arm. "That stunt you pulled with Nemesis, what were you trying to prove?"

"Ben, I . . ."

"And who cares anyway? Whatever it was, I think you proved it." And he shook Eddie by the hand. Warmly.

Eddie wondered briefly whether he might not still be in virtual reality. Ben Stanton shaking him by the hand? It couldn't be for real, could it? And here were Senior Tutor Grant and Corporal Keene, looking as though they were ready to join in on the congratulations. And the tech's voice reverberating through the chamber from the control room: "Binary bomb detonated.

Impact of antibinary particles successful. Virtual scenario and everything within eliminated." *Danger over. Threat removed. World saved. Too good to be true, right?*

Sadly, Eddie was correct.

The cybercradles started to shake, the mechanisms flashed and sparked as circuits overloaded.

"Are they supposed to do that?" Eddie wondered.

"Get back," Ben warned. Instinctively, Bond Team moved closer together. "What's happening?" he asked the nearest tech. "Does this have something to do with the bomb?"

The hapless tech didn't look like he had any idea.

But the cybercradles were rattling now, like something was inside them struggling to be let out, like something huge and powerful was restless to be born. The glass shields exploded. Bolts of searing light lanced the ceiling, driving everyone farther back. A shrill scream of release battered the eardrums.

A sound Bond Team had heard before.

"My God!" Jennifer realized with shock. "It's Nemesis! It's coming through!"

And it was. Within the pillars of light, the air darkened and danced in strange shapes and patterns, thickening into substance, shadowed and solidified.

In the virtual-reality chamber, a giant cybernetic spider was materializing.

"It's followed us," Jake gasped.

Followed him, Eddie thought woefully. Nemesis had been closest to him at the time of transfer. So he hadn't saved the world after all. He'd doomed it.

The stalks of the legs filled in, the bulging abdomen formed, the hideous black head took shape.

"This is impossible," someone said unhelpfully.

"Turn the power off!" Ben was suddenly shouting. "All of it. Shut everything down! It's feeding off the power and using it to materialize. Kill the power and kill Nemesis!"

Grant barked the order: "Power off! Now!"

The tech in the control room heard. And obeyed. The virtual-reality chamber was plunged into lifeless darkness. Nemesis screeched again. It was a shadow among shadows now, the cold stuff of nightmares.

"You're dead," Jennifer gloated.

Yet as it writhed and screamed and seemed to sense its unnatural life ebbing away, hatred drove Nemesis on. The creature glared at its enemies. Lori was certain she saw the evil glitter within its eyes. There was no time to run as Nemesis lunged toward them, its body fusing, crackling, and toppling. A massive, irresistible weight.

Lori cringed instinctively and threw up her hands.

And the falling form of Nemesis shattered against them, brittle and harmless. It was like a phantom, like a fume. Lori shuddered at the impact, as if she'd suddenly been shut in a freezer, but the effect was brief. Without the sustenance of electricity, without the nourishment of cyberspace, Nemesis could no longer exist. There was the echo of a final, futile howl, like distant static, like feedback.

Then Nemesis was no more.

"Can we get some lights back in here?" Grant's voice.

Lights flooded the chamber like hope. The cybercradles were ruined but they could be repaired. The important thing was that Nemesis had been destroyed. Bond Team looked at one another and hardly seemed able to believe it. For a second, there was silence. Then gleeful cries and an outbreak of hugging and backslapping. Even Corporal Keene seemed prepared to express solidarity, if a little gruffly.

Lori embraced Jake, who, alone among her teammates, seemed less than ecstatic, almost grim. She knew why. She squeezed his hands with secret meaning. Nemesis might have been eliminated, yes, but they still had one problem remaining.

It was time to deal with Simon Macey.

CHAPTER SIXTEEN

"I'm really glad you're okay, Lori," said Simon Macey. "I was really worried. I don't know what I'd have done if something had happened to you."

Drop dead, Macey, thought Lori. "Oh, Simon," she simpered. "Do you mean it?"

"Of course I mean it. You know how important you are to me."

Another day. Another clandestine rendezvous. Another classroom. But it ought to be on a stage, Lori thought. A theater would be an appropriate setting for a pair of such palpably false performances as this. If the spy game ever fell through, she and Simon both had a future in acting.

Here he was moving toward her, disarming her with that smile. His hands would be on her next, and she'd have to endure them. It was part of the plan. "In fact," said Simon, "when you were endangered by the Nemesis virus, it just made me realize I can't live without you. That's the truth."

"I believe you, Simon." *Like hell.*

The hands. On her shoulders. That smile leering like a mask inches from her face. She could probably break his nose from here and give him something to really smile about. *But keep the anger in, Lori. Play the Angel. Remember your lines.*

"And Simon, I feel the same."

"You do?"

"Being so close to death focused my mind, made me see things clearly. I saw you clearly, maybe for the first time." *You oily creep.* "I know now that it's you I want to be with. No, let me finish. I don't think it's fair to the others to let this out before Last Team Standing, but afterward, I want everyone to know about you and me."

"Oh, Lori," said Simon Macey, "afterward, they will."

There'd be an embrace now (and there was). She'd have to feel him pressing against her (she did). And his hands like a customs official frisking for drugs. Stroking the back of her neck, beneath her hair. And there was kissing, too, and a lot of it (at least she had mouthwash back in her room).

"Lori," said Simon Macey, "you don't know how happy you've made me."

Lori smiled innocently. "Simon," she said, "the best is yet to come."

"But he didn't say anything to persuade you to sabotage our efforts in Last Team Standing or to pass on information about tactics or anything like that?" Jake sat thoughtfully on Lori's bed.

"Nothing like that," Lori called from the bathroom, "unless I was so keen to get out of there that I missed it." She emerged wearing her bathrobe and toweling her wet hair. "I needed a shower. Something to wash off the stink of hypocrisy."

Jake tried not to notice too much of Lori's bare flesh. "Well, he has to be planning to use you somehow."

"Ain't that the truth. And it was very unpleasant, too." Lori wound the towel around her hair like a turban.

"He must have said something. He must have done something." Jake got up and paced the room. "Macey wouldn't have missed a golden opportunity like that."

"Am I making you uncomfortable, Jake? If you want to step outside, it won't take a second to put some clothes on."

"No, don't bother." Jake blinked as Lori raised her eyebrows amusedly. "I mean, we haven't got the time. I know Cally's still in the infirmary, but Jen could be back any minute, and she won't want to see me here, that's for sure."

"No? From what Cally told me about the dome, I thought you two might be on the point of becoming an item. You look good together."

Jake shrugged. "Try telling that to Jen. I mean, I like her, Lori, I like her a lot, but just when I think we're getting somewhere, some kind of weird alarm bell goes off in Jennifer's head, and the shutters come down, and it's like I've grown a second head or something. I don't understand her."

Lori sighed sympathetically. "Well, we all know that Jen has issues she has to sort out. I guess if we could trace their source back to her past somehow we could help her come to terms with them, but if I were you —"

"Wait! Lori." Jake snapped his fingers.

"What's —?"

"Where did Macey touch you?" Jake inspected Lori's bathrobed body like Sherlock Holmes himself scrutinizing for clues. "Exactly where?"

"Exactly just about everywhere," said Lori. "I don't know about license to kill. A license to take liberties, that's Simon. But I'm not sure I'm following you."

"It's got to be a part of you that you scarcely even see yourself."

"I beg your pardon?"

"You said the magic words," Jake grinned. *"Trace their source.* That's how Macey's going to use you in Last Team Standing.

He's planted a tracer on you. You'll be giving away our position, and you won't even know it."

"But I'd have noticed . . ."

"Not necessarily." Jake's sharp eyes narrowed. "Lean your head forward, like you're nodding off to sleep in one of Grant's History of Espionage lessons. That's it." He pored over the delicate skin of Lori's exposed neck, pushed the towel up to analyze the very roots of her hair. Jake laughed. "I knew it. I knew it!"

"What? Blond's my natural color."

"No. Feel this. Feel the back of your neck." He helped to guide Lori's fingers to the black dot smaller than a fingernail that was affixed to skin which would normally be hidden by her hair. "It *is* a tracer. I was right. Lori, my dear, you've been bugged."

"Well, get it off me then," Lori complained. "I've got a few ideas where I can stick it on Simon Macey, and all of them are painful."

"I don't think so." Jake patted Lori's neck and the tracer. "This little beauty stays where it is."

"What? Why? So sleazy Simon can monitor my every move?"

"Exactly," Jake schemed darkly. "Macey thinks he's got you where he wants you. Let him think it. 'Cause when Last Team Standing starts, he's gonna find it's the other way around."

"What, no grapes?" Eddie rummaged through Cally's bedside table. "You can't be a proper hospital patient without grapes. I'm afraid it looks like you're going to have to leave and rejoin Bond Team, Cal."

"Funny," grinned Cally, propped up by an extraordinary

number of pillows. "That's pretty much exactly what the doctor said on his rounds just a half hour ago."

"Really?" Lori and Jennifer were perched on either side of Cally's bed while the three boys stood. "That's great news."

"Did he actually say you could return to active training?" Ben was more cautious. He was thinking about the day after tomorrow and Last Team Standing. It wasn't called that for nothing. Last Team Lying in a Hospital Bed wouldn't work.

Cally, though, was emphatic. "He actually did, Ben. Said it'd be the best thing for me, and I agree. There wasn't much physically wrong with me anyway, nothing that a few days of rest hasn't cured. It was only my mind that Nemesis was trying to mess with."

"If only there were a few boys like that," Lori observed facetiously.

"I don't think Nemesis was quite sure what to make of me," Cally said. "Grant thinks that's why I was kept alive in the VR scenario. Nemesis was probing my mind, trying to work me out."

"It should have known better," joked Eddie. "Nobody can work a woman out."

Jake and Jennifer exchanged a glance that could have meant anything.

"I think it had given up, anyway," Cally continued. "If you hadn't come when you did, guys, my mind would have been mush."

"What?" Ben said. "You mean like Eddie's?"

"Oh, that's cruel," Eddie complained.

"I've got a lot to thank you for, all of you." Cally squeezed Lori's and Jennifer's arms.

"Bond Team looks after its own," said Ben.

"I feel a pep talk coming on," mouthed Jake.

"And now that we're all together again, and all declared fit, we'd better start focusing on our tactics for Last Team Standing."

Ben never missed a trick, Jake thought, in a kind of grudging admiration.

"I hope I don't need to remind anyone how important this final event is," Ben continued. "Palmer and Hannay teams have already been eliminated, so it's us against Macey's lot, and we can only win the Sherlock Shield if we take them in Last Team Standing. We're close, but we're not there yet."

"Don't worry about it, Ben," said Jennifer. "The day we can't beat Solo Team one on one is the day we deserve to get mind-wiped and sent home."

"I'm glad you're confident, Jen," Ben approved, "but don't forget the scores. Because of the Skyscapes debacle —" Lori registered with gratitude that Ben didn't mention the Gun Run — "Solo Team is ahead. Not by much, maybe, but it gives them an edge. What it boils down to is that we can't afford a single casualty. We have to eliminate every one of Macey's lot without losing a life ourselves. So we need to be sharp, and I mean *sharp.*"

"Any sharper, leader man," said Eddie, "and I'd be cutting myself."

"Very funny, Eddie." Ben regarded his teammates warningly. "But Macey's going to do whatever he can to win, by fair means or foul, and don't you forget it."

Lori's eyes met Jake's. They wouldn't.

Grant had introduced the Last Team Standing event as the modern equivalent of the late-twentieth-century craze for paint guns in the forest. He'd shown them old footage of long-dead executives with fat bellies and boiler suits wheezing from one tree to another and firing paint balls at each other with all the accuracy of blind men in the fog. At night. The purpose of the exercise had apparently been to foster a sense of corporate identity and teamwork. The latter was still part of the thinking behind Last Team Standing, and the showdown between Spy High's two leading teams also took place in the real world — no virtual reality or special effects here — but boiler suits had been exchanged for shock suits and paint guns superceded by stasis rifles. The idea remained the same: to stop the opposing team in its tracks, if not dead, then at least temporarily paralyzed. And there was one hour in which to do it.

The members of Bond Team checked their weapons as a series of metal posts rose from the ground behind them to a height of about four yards. Lights flashed along each post's length, signifying that the energy fence that marked out the limits of the game space was activated. Brushing into that invisible barrier now, either accidentally or for some unfair purpose, would earn the culprit not only a nasty shock but also immediate expulsion from the event. The competing teams had only a limited area, most of it heavily wooded, in which to outwit their opponents.

"Right. Three teams of two," announced Ben. "Me and Lori. Jake and Jennifer. Cally and Eddie." Nobody said otherwise, although Jake couldn't help notice Jennifer scowl sulkily. Whatever he'd done wrong, she still hadn't forgiven him. "Watch each other's backs. We don't want Macey's bunch to get behind us."

"It's the kind of sneaky, lowdown trick they'll go in for," disapproved Eddie.

"We want to get behind them."

"Great tactics, Ben," Eddie enthused.

"Each pair keep within sight of the others. We don't want to get separated. And you know the call if anybody sees anything."

Everybody nodded. "Communicators would help," Lori noted.

"Yeah, but no electronic aids allowed," Ben said, "of any kind."

Not even tracers, Lori reflected. She felt the back of her neck gingerly, the tiny device like a blister on her skin. Jake winked at her encouragingly.

"Okay," Ben finished. "Solo Team will be entering the game space from the other side by now. Let's give 'em something to worry about."

Bond Team delved into the woodland. Jennifer and Jake took the right, Cally and Eddie the left, while Ben and Lori kept the central position. They moved silently, stealthily, senses sharply alert for the slightest sign of human company. The Sherlock Shield depended on the outcome of the next sixty minutes.

Lori saw the intensity on Ben's face, his total commitment to the cause. She could never tell him about Simon Macey and her, never. And she could never tell him that it didn't matter how they crept and crouched and crawled through the forest, Solo Team was going to be bearing down on them with unerring precision thanks to the little bit of help Simon had slapped to the back of her neck. And even if Jake's plan worked here and now, what was to stop Simon from revealing the whole truth to Ben and ruining her life that way? She saw her boyfriend regarding her with concern. "Don't worry," he whispered. She wished.

To the left: "You all right, Cal?" Eddie asked, looking out for his teammate. "We can kind of have a rest if you need to."

"I'm not an invalid," Cally retorted, though her limbs already felt heavy, slow.

"No, I didn't mean . . ."

"I know you didn't." Cally corrected her tone. "But I'm doing fine. How could I not? I've got the spy with a smile for my partner."

And when she smiled at him, Eddie found he didn't care whether they won the Sherlock Shield or not.

To the right: "Listen, Jen." Jake not being able to bear the silence between them. "I know this isn't the time or the place, but afterward, I mean later, we've really got to talk, sort ourselves out."

"You're right, Jake," agreed Jennifer coldly.

"I am?"

"This isn't the time or the place." Her face was closed against him.

Jake sighed. Well, he'd tried. He hoped his plan for the tracer would be more successful. He judged that it was time.

For no apparent reason, Jake made the call of a bird.

Jennifer ducked as low as if it had been the whistle of a bomb. "What do you think you're doing?"

"I think I see someone," Jake hissed, taking cover. "Over there." He indicated just about the entire forest and emphasized his belief with a second birdcall.

"What are you talking about?" Jennifer squinted into the green distance. "There's nobody over there. Where exactly?"

But it didn't matter now. Jake's real aim had been achieved. The rest of Bond Team squatted down alongside him and Jennifer, stasis rifles primed. Jake caught Lori's eye ever so subtly and nodded. While the others craned forward, eager to glimpse the enemy, she lagged behind. Nobody noticed her hand apparently massaging the back of her neck.

"What have you got, Jake?" Ben was demanding.

"Macey and Sonia Dark," Jake lied. "I'm sure it was them, at least them."

"I didn't see anything, Ben." Jennifer wasn't happy. "There's nothing."

Ben peered out into the forest. Certainly looked like nothing, but did he want to take chances? Was a good leader the one who took risks or the one who played the percentages? Jake wasn't usually given to flights of fancy.

"I'm telling you," he stressed. "Simon. Sonia. Maybe all of Solo Team. Coming our way." Another surreptitious glance at Lori. This time, it was her turn to nod.

"Well . . ." Ben couldn't afford mistakes.

"Ben, there's nothing there." Jennifer seemed just as convinced as Jake.

"I saw something, too," claimed Lori. "It has to be Solo Team."

Jennifer snapped around to glare at Lori. Of course she would support Jake, even though for some unfathomable reason they were both clearly lying. But Lori's intervention had convinced Ben.

"Okay, we'll fall back," he planned. "We'll form a defensive semicircle on the other side of this side of open ground. If they haven't seen us, maybe we can pick one or two of them off. Let's do it."

Bond Team retreated, spaced themselves out, and created an arc enclosing the perfect killing ground, if anyone was unlucky enough to wander into it. With her tracer now removed and adorning the undergrowth, Lori reasoned, the chances of that were good. *Bring 'em on. Bring 'em all on.*

They didn't have long to wait. "What did I tell you?" grinned Jake, he didn't dare look at Lori in case he burst into triumphant laughter.

"I don't believe it," gaped Jennifer.

But there was no denying it now. Stealing between the trees at the limits of their vision, but moving inexorably closer, were not only Simon, not only Sonia Dark, but all six members of Solo Team — present, correct, and about to be put out of their misery. All of Bond Team's trigger fingers tightened on their stasis rifles.

"What are they doing?" Ben murmured, largely to himself. "They're all bunched up together. They're making themselves easy targets." Was it some sort of trick? He wouldn't put deceit of any sort past Simon Macey, but Ben found it impossible to guess what advantage Solo Team could gain from keeping so close to each other.

Ben shook his head in bafflement. "Christmas must be early this year."

"Yeah," added Jake, "and here come the turkeys."

Yelling at the tops of their voices, Solo Team charged. Their rifles crackled, stasis bolts lancing through the innocent forest air.

"They haven't seen us. They can't have seen us. What's going on?" Cally turned to Eddie.

"Maybe they don't like the look of that bush," Eddie suggested, "the one they're blowing to bits."

"Wait for it," hissed Ben. "Let them come on a little farther." Then he'd have Macey in his sights.

Solo Team stopped. They seemed stunned, stupefied. Simon Macey looked at something in his hand, shook it vigorously. Solo Team clustered around him.

This was as good as it was going to get.

"Fire!" cried Ben.

A barrage of stasis bolts ripped through Solo Team. They didn't even have time to raise their own rifles. Huxley was paralyzed instantly, stiffening and toppling, out of the game. So was Johns. Conrad caught fire from the front and rear, jerked, spun, fell.

Bond Team was on its feet now, sensing total victory.

But they weren't encircling the enemy, not entirely. Simon saw his chance. He grabbed Sonia Dark. She swore and she struggled, but neither were helpful. She took the stasis bolt intended for Simon. Then he let her go, sprinting away as she fell, his stasis rifle forgotten, a reckless fugitive.

Out of range.

"Damnit!" spat Ben. "Let's get after him."

"No!" Jake's urgency made everyone pause. The blaze in his eyes brooked no contradiction. "Macey's mine."

Simon's panic was making him stumble, slowing him down, and he wasn't thinking straight, either. What had gone wrong with the tracer? Everything had been working so perfectly, and now he was blundering about in the forest, a team of one. And he could hear a pursuer. It'd be Stanton, stasis rifle at the ready to claim his victory. And without his own weapon — why had he dropped it? Stupid! There was nothing he could do to prevent it.

But he could sure take the gloss off. Maybe it was time Stanton learned the truth about his pretty little girlfriend.

Simon slowed to a halt, raised his hands in surrender, turned to face Ben Stanton with a sneer. Which quickly became a frown. It wasn't Stanton, after all. Instead, that reject Domer, Daly. Who didn't seem to be slowing down. "All right, I give up." Jake kept coming. "I said I give up, are you deaf?"

Jake powered into Simon Macey, and the two of them thudded to the ground.

"What do you think you're doing, you moron?" Simon writhed but Jake was on top of him, fists bunched. "I give up! Just shoot me, and end it."

"Not yet, scumbag. We need to talk. Actually, I need to talk, and you need to listen."

"What? You're . . . insane!" Simon blurted. "This is against the rules!"

"Yeah?" Jake thrust his face closer to Macey's. His eyes burned with rage that could have scorched the foliage. "Well, so is planting a tracer on a member of another team."

Macey blanched. His lips quivered. "I did no such thing. You can't —"

"No lies, Macey — just listen!" Jake clamped his hands around Simon's throat. "I know about you and Lori. I know you've been using her and exploiting her. And in my book, buddy, that's lower than dirt, and where I come from, that's worth the kind of pounding I'd really like to give you now."

"Get . . . off . . . me!"

"But I'm going to be reasonable with you, Macey, just this once. You can keep your good looks. You can keep your teeth in nice even rows. But if you *ever* open your mouth to anyone — I don't mean just Ben, I mean *anyone* — about what you did to Lori, *ever*, then one dark night when you least expect it, you and

me are going to meet again, and then I'm not going to be reasonable, and you won't be charming anyone else for a very long
time. Do you understand me?"

A kind of gurgle came out of Simon Macey. Throttling
tends to impair the communication.

"I can't hear you." Jake reluctantly let go of Macey's throat.
"Do you understand?"

". . . Yes . . . *yes!* I . . . understand . . ." Simon coughed fit-
fully.

"Good. Then it looks like we're just about done here."

Just in time, too. "Jake, what's going on?" The others had arrived.

"Oh, nothing. Nothing important." Jake got to his feet and
hauled Simon Macey to his. "Simon had a little bit of a fall, that's
all. And he's got something he wants to say to you, haven't you,
Simon?"

Lori's eyes widened in sudden alarm.

"What is it, Macey?"

Simon shared his defeated glare between Jake and Ben.
Pointedly, he didn't even glance at Lori. "Yeah, I've got something to say. I give up. It's all over, Stanton, the Sherlock Shield's
yours."

The ceremony was exactly as Ben had imagined.

The whole school, teachers and students alike, had assembled in the Hall of Heroes. Grant was there, of course, and so was Corporal Keene, in the uniform he obviously kept clean for noncombat occasions. Lacey Bannon, Mr. Korita, even old Gadge, who clearly had no idea why but at least refrained from talking to the wall during the speeches. A special screen had been installed for Jonathan Deveraux's contribution. All of the student teams sat on one side of the Hall, with those Spy High graduates not otherwise occupied on missions sitting behind them.

Only Bond Team sat apart from its peers. Because only Bond Team was there to be awarded the Sherlock Shield.

Ben didn't listen much to the speeches from Deveraux and from Grant. All the talk of honor and achievement, of setting standards and living up to examples — it wasn't that he disagreed with it or even that he'd heard it all before. Ben simply wanted to enjoy the moment, to revel in it, to imprint the scene so indelibly on his mind that it would seem as if it might last forever.

The admiring gaze of the graduates whose ranks he'd one day be joining, the envious eyes of Hannay, Palmer, and Solo Teams — especially Solo Team, with Simon Macey in particular looking like he'd swallowed a lemon with more to come. This was right. This was good. This was why he'd joined Spy High.

When Grant called for "Benjamin T. Stanton Jr., the leader

of Bond Team," to step forward and collect the Sherlock Shield, Ben could have done it with his eyes closed. He'd rehearsed this moment countless times in the privacy of his own head. The reality didn't disappoint.

"Thank you, sir," Ben said. He shook Grant's hand (or did Grant shake his?). He took hold of the Sherlock Shield. He held it high. He accepted the applause as his just deserts. When they made the film of his life . . .

The others joined him, a little unnecessarily, he thought. There were smiles all around, hugging, backslapping, and general congratulations.

Correction: Smiles *nearly* all around.

Jennifer could have been on the same diet as Simon Macey. She wasn't enjoying the audience's adulation at all. Her eyes were darting to the exits as if she was considering making a break for one of them any second. *Unstable, Ben reflected, definitely unstable, but at least she hadn't dragged the team down.*

Whatever Jennifer's problem was, it couldn't hurt them now.

Later that evening, the girls were preparing themselves for the Sherlock Shield Ball. All six members of Bond Team, needless to say, were the guests of honor, and Cally and Lori were planning their outfits and appearance with all the precision of a field operation. Jennifer, on the other hand, was not. Jennifer seemed to be doing nothing but sitting cross-legged on her bed and staring grimly into space.

"You not feeling well, Jen?" Cally asked.

"I'm fine." Each word like a window shutter slammed.

"Then why aren't you getting changed?" Lori wondered. "The party'll start without us."

"I'm not going to the party," Jennifer said, with a scorn that stopped both her teammates in their tracks.

"You're not? Why?"

"Oh, I wouldn't want to cramp your style, Lori. Wouldn't want to get in your way."

"What?" Lori didn't understand. Where was Jennifer's sudden vitriol coming from? "What do you mean?"

"Nothing."

Lori looked for support from Cally, who shrugged, mystified. "Wait a minute, Jen, you can't make a pointed comment like that and then just say, 'nothing.' Have we got a problem I'm not aware of?"

"As if you don't know," Jennifer snapped petulantly.

"I *don't* know," Lori claimed. "Enlighten me. Cal, do you have any idea — ?"

"Jake. It's Jake. You and Jake."

"What do you mean, *me and Jake*? It's me and Ben, Jen, haven't you noticed by now? Blond guy, tall, leader of Bond Team, actually. Jake's just —"

"Someone you exchange meaningful glances with," Jennifer accused. "Someone you secretly meet on the grounds."

"Oh." Either she and Jake had been careless, or Lori could quite understand why Jennifer deserved her place at Spy High.

"Yes. Oh," said Jennifer.

"Lori?" Cally regarded her teammate quizzically.

"Listen, Jen, you've got it all wrong." Lori launched into the truth-but-not-the-whole-truth explanation. "What you saw . . . I had a bit of a problem. Jake was the only one who could help me out. And he did. He helped me sort myself out. As a friend. That's it. There's nothing else, nothing romantic, if that's what you're worried about. Ben's my boyfriend. You can see that, can't you?" Jennifer looked as if she couldn't see that. "Listen," Lori tried a different approach, "it's you Jake likes, Jen. He told me so himself."

"You see?" Cally joined forces with Lori. "What did I tell you before? You mean you didn't talk to him?"

Jennifer's hostility began to waver. "I was going to, but then I saw . . . and then I thought . . . So I was really horrible to him." She regarded her teammates with dismay. "Jake's going to hate me now, isn't he?"

"Oh, I don't know," Lori pondered. "I bet if you do something, like swing by the boy's room right now, and hint that you're available to be escorted to the party, Jake might be persuaded to volunteer. Like drooling, tongue-hanging-out, kind of persuaded."

"You think so?" Jennifer laughed. She was suddenly a different person.

"We think so," Cally confirmed.

"I guess I'd better go, then." Before she lost her courage again. "See you in a bit. And Lori, Cally." Jennifer smiled. "Thanks."

Cally watched her leave. "The path of true love never runs smoothly," she observed. "Now Lo, what was this problem that only Jake could help you with?"

Jennifer ran along the corridors. She had the crazy idea that if she didn't get to Jake absolutely as soon as possible something would happen, and she'd never see him again. Certain events in her life that haunted her dreams had made her pessimistic, bleak, but here was a chance for something good, something positive. And now that the business with Lori was cleared up, no one could stand in her way.

Except maybe Senior Tutor Elmore Grant, whom she nearly knocked off of his artificial feet. "Hey, where's the fire?" He wasn't taking it personally.

"Sorry, sir. I need to . . . see someone."

"Me, too, coincidentally. You, Jennifer." He handed her an envelope, addressed to "Jennifer Chen at Deveraux Academy." "This came for you today. I meant to give it to you earlier, but what with the ceremony and everything . . . we don't get much actual mail these days, do we? All e-mail and videophones. Modern life. I supp — are you all right, Jennifer?"

"Yes, of course." But she wasn't. "Thank you. For this." It was from Aunt Li. She recognized the writing. It couldn't be good news.

"Well, I expect I'll see you at the party, then, Jennifer."

She didn't reply. She never saw Grant leave. The world around her darkened, dimmed, and she could only see the letter. Jennifer fumbled the envelope open. Aunt Li did not waste ink. *He's back.*

Of course he was. Of course. Jennifer felt that she couldn't breathe, couldn't stand, couldn't think. She groped to the wall for support. *He's back.* She knew he would be someday. It just happened to be today.

She felt the gorge rising in her throat, but there was nothing to be done. Tears stung her eyes. No time for Jake now. Only time for one thing.

"So are we a happy boy this evening?" Lori finally managed to break away from Ben and have a word with Jake between songs.

She was mildly surprised that he wasn't up and dancing like everyone else. She was more than mildly surprised that he was alone.

"What do you mean? The Shield? I guess if Ben shares the credit around . . ."

"No, dummy. Jennifer. You know? Tall, dark, and gorgeous? Where is she?"

"I hoped you were gonna tell me," Jake admitted. "Isn't she with you?"

Lori frowned. A sneaking sense of foreboding crawled like an insect up her spine. "She was supposed to be coming to see you in your room, to ask you to the party."

"She didn't." Jake matched Lori's concern. "I haven't seen her since the ceremony. When was this?"

"Ages ago. I mean, Cal and I thought you'd gone off together or something. She never came back. You really haven't seen her?" Lori scanned the room for Jennifer in vain.

"No," Jake said. "And trust me, I've looked."

The music started playing again, loudly. Ben was waiting for Lori to rejoin him on the dance floor. Cally and Eddie seemed to be practicing wrestling holds. Suddenly, Lori didn't feel much like socializing. Something was wrong.

"Maybe she changed her mind. Maybe she's just gone back to your room."

"Maybe." Lori nodded thoughtfully. "I think I'll go and check. You want to come?"

"Try stopping me."

"Hey, Ben," called Eddie, as he watched a confused Ben stare after Lori and Jake who were rushing from the room. "I'd look out if I were you. Could be you're losing your touch!"

*   *   *

"Jennifer? Jen? Are you in here?"

The fact that Lori had to turn on the lights suggested otherwise.

"So where is she, then?"

"Wait, Jake. Look. A note." Lori retrieved the single leaf of folded paper from the middle of Jennifer's bed. She read it. She paled.

"Well?" prompted Jake. "What does it say?"

"She's gone, Jake."

"What do you mean? Gone where?"

Lori's expression was grave, final. "Jennifer's gone."

THE FUTURE IS FANGED . . .

Turn the page for a sneak peek at

SPY HIGH:
MISSION THREE

THE SERPENT
SCENARIO

Arriving Fall 2004 from
Little, Brown and Company

While Spy High is different from most other schools in almost every way, it is still customary in the small hours of the morning for its students to be in their beds and sound asleep. It's unusual for five of them to be congregated in one room together, and certainly for anybody to be packing as if for immediate departure. Which was what Jake seemed to be doing.

"At the risk of repeating myself one final time," Ben said, "this is a very dumb idea."

"At the risk of repeating myself also," replied Jake, "you don't really want to know how little I care, do you, Ben?"

"Stop squabbling, you two," scolded Cally. "We're supposed to be a team, remember?"

"There was a time we acted like it," Ben said. "Now everybody's running off pursuing their own agendas."

Jake threw a final item of clothing into his case as if he preferred to be aiming at Ben's head. "Listen, Stanton, what else is there to do? We've got a good idea where Jennifer's gone, half a good idea as to why, and we can't just leave her to it. Doing nothing is not an option."

"We could tell Grant." But even Ben felt that was a lame, somehow sneaky thing to say or do. "Or I guess not," he corrected himself.

"Jen's a member of Bond Team," said Lori. "Bond Team looks after its own."

"You can look after me any day, Lo," teased Eddie. "Hey, and Jakey, don't forget your deodorant. It's hot on the coast."

"Leaving the rest of us to face the flak." Ben wasn't finished yet. "Maybe disciplinary procedures."

"That's typical of you, Stanton," scoffed Jake. "Not bothered about Jennifer at all, just what might happen to you, a blot on the perfect record."

"Jake," Lori snapped. "That's not fair."

Jake relented a little. Maybe he had gone too far. He just wanted to be away, after Jennifer. Whatever was going to happen was going to happen. "All right. Okay. Uncalled for. But Ben, if it was Lori missing, Lori maybe in trouble, wouldn't you be the first to do what I'm doing now?"

Ben hung his head. He didn't feel it was a reasonable question to be asked with Lori present. "If you put it like that," he felt obliged to say. "You go, Jake. We'll cover for you. Like Lori said, Bond Team looks after its own."

"Another moving Kleenex moment," said Eddie.

Lori accompanied Jake to one of the college's side doors. It hadn't been thought wise for them all to traipse through the corridor at three in the morning.

"This is it, then," Jake said softly. "Cab should be waiting outside the grounds. Cally's hacked me onto a flight to LA. I'll call you when I find Jennifer."

"Make sure you do, Jake," Lori returned. Because they were both whispering, they were very close together. She could feel his breath on her cheek. "I hope you find what else you're looking for, too. With Jennifer. You deserve your happiness."

"You reckon so?"

"All that help you gave me with Simon Macey? I know so. Good luck, Jake."

"Thanks, Lori." And they hugged. For quite a long time.

When she finally turned away from watching Jake become invisible in the darkness, Lori found that her eyes were filled with tears.

* * *

Someone had once said that schooldays were the best days of your life. Whoever it was had obviously never been to school in Undertown, Los Angeles. The crumbling heaps of bricks and mortar with Jennifer Chen waiting outside seemed more like the remains of a war zone than an educational institution. Students slunk between them like terrorists; she half-expected to see the teachers wearing flak jackets. If you were looking for a stimulating learning experience, it seemed you'd better look elsewhere, maybe toward the glittering, lofty towers of Uptown that could be glimpsed faintly and far off, like an unobtainable dream, like a hope for the future that could never come true. Jennifer set her lips grimly. If a Selector from Deveraux hadn't seen her and spotted her potential, if Senior Tutor Grant hadn't approached her with the offer of a place at Spy High, she'd maybe be attending this very school, her life chances as dilapidated as its buildings.

But she'd taken her place. She'd trained at Spy High. And now she was going to use that training for the purpose she'd always intended, revenge on the man who'd killed her family.

She wondered if she'd recognize Kim when the school day ended and the students left. It had been a while. They'd promised to always keep in touch. To be best friends, *"Best friends forever."* But after the murders, Jennifer had moved away to live with Aunt Li and Uncle Fung. Then she'd moved farther away from Kim to the East Coast and Deveraux Academy. Distances that, perhaps, were not only literal.

In Jennifer's mind she could see two little Chinese girls in identical clothes, with identical smiles, holding hands and skipping in the street. "You sure you aren't sisters, you two?" old

Mrs. Koerner had said, her sight dim behind her glasses, as the young Kim and Jennifer giggled. "You're more like sisters."

Kim might look slightly different now — as Jennifer did herself — but nothing could eradicate the past. Jennifer needed help, and she trusted Kim to supply it.

The school bell screamed like an air-raid siren. Students scattered, pelting past Jennifer as if they expected bombs to start falling any second. Jennifer stood her ground and watched. Kim had been nine years old the last time they'd talked. Five years of change. She doubted there'd be pigtails now, or little white socks, or a doll hanging from her hand.

She was right. There were none of those things. Kim Tang wore the typically loose, shapeless garments of the teenager, her ink-black hair that had once been longer than Jennifer's was now cropped short like some kind of penance, and she held not a toy in her hand but a cigarette, which she smoked with the automatic regularity born of much practice.

A pang of nostalgia squeezed Jennifer's heart.

"Kim!" she called out. "Kim!"

Her old friend heard. For a moment her expression seemed fearful, haunted. Then she saw Jennifer running toward her and for another moment there was blankness. But maybe a moment after five years wasn't bad. Next would come the "Great to see you."

"Jennifer? What are you doing in a hole like this?"

"If we keep on like this maybe they'll give us season tickets," Eddie had said. Being summoned to Grant's study did seem to be becoming a habit for Bond Team. Each time there was a little more room for them to fit in. Because each time there seemed to be fewer members of Bond Team.

They'd tried to keep Jake's absence undetected for as long as possible. They'd told Ms. Bannon at Weapons Instruction that they hadn't seen Jake yet that morning but he was probably in the infirmary because he hadn't been feeling too well last night — he'd said so. Ms. Bannon had shrugged and turned her attention back to laser-guided pulse rifles. They'd told Senior Tutor Grant the same story in History of Espionage. Grant, however, perhaps demonstrating why he was Senior Tutor, immediately contacted the infirmary and learned that not only was Jake Daly not languishing in a bed there now, but had not felt the need to consult a member of the medical staff since before Christmas, and then only because of a slightly sprained ankle.

Hence the meeting in Grant's study.

It was worse than before, Ben knew that. This time Jonathan Deveraux himself was directly involved, the screen on the tutor's desk displaying his grave and finely sculpted features. As usual, there was no personal appearance from the academy's founder, and Ben sought to take heart from that. Surely, if this was going to be an expulsion matter, even the notoriously reclusive Mr. Deveraux, whom no student had ever seen in the flesh, would physically be there to take charge? On the other hand, though, the founder's cool and clinical gaze upon them was worrying enough.

"So," said Deveraux, in a tone pitched midway between accusation and amusement, "to misplace one team member is unfortunate, but to misplace two beings to seem like carelessness."

"It's my fault, sir, my responsibility." Ben raised his impressively square chin and tried to look noble. The trouble with being team leader, he thought, was that now and again he had to act like one. "I should have known Jake might do something like this."

"Something like what, Stanton?" Deveraux's diamond-chipped eyes narrowed.

"Well, he's gone after Jennifer, hasn't he?" Was the founder testing him? Surely they'd assumed that much. "I mean, that's what we . . . why else would he just up and leave?"

"You may very well be right, Stanton," said Deveraux, "but Daly gave you no indication that he was planning to depart, for whatever reason?"

"No, sir," Ben lied, guilt forcing his eyes downward.

"Not to any of us, sir," Lori supported.

"Absolutely not." Cally, too.

"He never talks to me about anything." Eddie made the ignorance unanimous.

"Such great loyalty to his teammate," observed Deveraux, "if Daly has indeed risked his future at Spy High in order to pursue Jennifer Chen, as you all believe. A loyalty that I can see extends throughout Bond Team."

Was that sarcasm? Ben wondered. Did Deveraux realize that they weren't telling the truth? What did he know?

"Is there anything else you'd like to tell us?"

Oh, yeah, Ben thought. *We also hacked into the academy's confidential personal files, and did you know that Jen's family was slaughtered by a street gang?* "No, sir," he said. "Nothing."

"Then this meeting is terminated," Deveraux said.

"Sir?" Lori. "About Jake, sir, and Jennifer too, I suppose. What's going to happen now?"

The wryest of smiles played around the founder's lips. "Now," he said, "only time will tell."

* * *

"He knows," Ben groaned, throwing himself back on his bed. "Deveraux knows everything. He's bound to. We're dead."

"You think?" Eddie shook his head mournfully. "And I had such a great future."

"Don't be too sure," Cally cautioned.

"What? About my future?"

"Eddie, why don't you suddenly adopt meditation as a hobby, like, immediately? I mean about Deveraux. He might have his suspicions but he can't be certain. Neither can Grant. I covered our tracks pretty well on the system. Nobody'll even know we've been in."

"You hope," Ben said gloomily.

"I was proud of you back there, Ben." Lori tried to lighten the mood. "Taking the blame on yourself like that. If Jake knew, I'm sure he'd appreciate it."

She failed.

"Oh, great. Excellent." Ben laughed at the absurdity of it all. "So we all of us talk our way into a mind-wipe and you're 'sure' that Jake will 'appreciate it.' Well, that makes me feel a lot better, Lori. Hope it docs the same for you." Jake and even Jennifer had never exactly been Ben's favorite members of Bond Team. He was struggling not to feel aggrieved by the situation their actions seemed to have forced him into. "I hope it keeps you warm at night. Because after we're expelled, when we wake up one morning and can't remember each other or ever having met or been here at Spy High at all, let's hope that a little bit of Jake's appreciation'll make the sacrifice worthwhile. Me, though, I have my doubts."

* * *

There hadn't been hugs but that was okay. It didn't mean any-thing. Kim probably felt a little too self-conscious to express her feelings physically in front of new friends who'd never seen Jennifer before. Kim hadn't seen her in years. She was bound to be surprised.

"You've come back, Jen." Staggered would be more like it. Incredulous. As if Jennifer had pulled a Lazarus and risen from the dead. "Why?"

"We need to talk, Kim. I'll explain everything. But hey, it's good to see you again."

They went to Gaudini's, of course, just the two of them. There'd been a time when the coffee bar had seemed the epit-ome of glitz and glamour to the two girls from Undertown, when the golden letters of its name, inscribed so dashingly across its glittering windows, had suggested both drama and romance, where discreet tables and quiet corners had promised secret encounters with a grown-up world that neither Jennifer nor Kim had yet experienced. Now the name was peeling and faded, the interior poky, dusty, like a wonderful present left too long and forgotten. Mr. Gaudini himself looked too old still to be working, and the coffee he served them came in chipped cups and had dripped into the saucers.

Jennifer sighed. Another illusion shattered. But at least she could still rely on Kim. "Where do you want to sit?"

"Gee, I don't know. We might have a wait," said Kim sarcas-tically. The girls were Gaudini's only customers.

"Place has seen better days," Jennifer observed as they chose a corner table.

"Hasn't everywhere?" retorted Kim. "Hasn't everyone?"

"What are you talking about? Looking good, Kim."

"Need laser treatment on the eyes, Jen. I'm looking like crap. My mirror lets me know every morning. You remember old Mrs. Koerner never used to be able to tell us apart?" For a second the ghost of a smile fluttered at Kim's lips. She gazed at Jennifer's glossy tide of hair, her perfect oval face. "Don't reckon she'd have the same problem now, do you? Mind if I smoke?" Jennifer didn't. "Want one?" Didn't again. "You still at that posh school I heard you went to? What was it? Dev something?"

"Deveraux. The Deveraux Academy."

"Hmm. Bet there's no smoking at Deveraux, right?" Kim took a deep drag of her cigarette, like she half-wanted to choke herself. "Why aren't you there now? Holiday or something?"

"Not quite."

"Not gotten expelled, have you?"

"Not yet." Jennifer smiled mysteriously.

"Little bit of a rebel still, is it?" Kim nodded in approval. "So why *are* you here, Jen? It is kind of nostalgic to see you, girl-friend, don't get me wrong, but why now? I've got a feeling it's not just for old time's sake."

"Oh, it is, Kim." Jennifer's expression darkened. "Just not the old times you mean."

Kim understood. "Your parents."

"And Shang. Don't forget my baby brother. He'd be eleven next month if, well, you know. *If.*"

"Look, Jen, I can't begin to understand how you must have felt when it happened, how you must feel now, but coming back to Undertown, I don't see how that's going to help. You should be letting the scars heal, not tearing open old wounds."

Jennifer leaned forward eagerly, intensely. "I've got information," she said, "about the man who did it."

Now it was Kim's expression that darkened. Identical, like they'd been as children. "Don't go there, Jen," she warned. "Don't even think of going there. Whatever you think you know, forget it. You can't change the past, no one can, and it sounds like you've got some sort of future to look forward to at this school, which is more than the rest of us have. Don't risk throwing that away by getting in over your head back here. Listen, Jen, you want my advice?"

"I want your help, Kim."

"My advice is leave now and don't look back. You don't belong here anymore, Jen. You don't know what it's like."

Jennifer opened her mouth, but whether to protest or agree Kim never found out. At that moment the great glass window of Gaudini's exploded inward, spraying the restaurant with jagged shards like shavings of ice. Kim screamed, threw herself against the back wall. Jennifer also jumped to her feet, but only to assume a defensive stance. Her Spy High training worked just as well in Undertown as anywhere else.

And she might be needing it. Two youths, barely out of their teens, leaped through the gaping hole in the window, male and female, maybe a couple. They certainly seemed to have a lot in common. Black clothes. White skin. White like frost or death or the flag of surrender. Bloodshot eyes. Blood-red lips. Hands like claws. And teeth. Jennifer registered them as thin lips peeled back in a chilling parody of a smile. Teeth like the cutting edge of a hacksaw. The intruders recognized fear in Gaudini's. They enjoyed it. They seemed to want to add to it.

"Jen, watch out!"

Jennifer didn't really need Kim's warning, though she appreciated the sentiment. The male youth was rushing directly at her, his movement jerky, convulsive, as though some kind of current was coursing through him. He was quick but clumsy. A hopeless attack. Jennifer smacked her fist into his torso, shuddered at the impact. Her assailant halted in mid-charge. Dazed, he might have collapsed anyway. Jennifer's second blow helped him on his way.

"Wow, Jennifer!" gaped Kim, and then: "Gaudini!"

But Mr. Gaudini evidently did not require assistance in dealing with the second youth. From under the counter he whipped an old pump-action stasis rifle, fired it point blank at the girl like he knew what he was doing. She cried out, shuddered as the paralysis took swift effect, fell to the floor stiffly. And didn't get up.

"You kids all right?" said Mr. Gaudini.

"Yeah, thanks. We're fine." Jennifer was already kneeling by the unconscious form of her attacker, inspecting him more closely.

"Okay. I'm calling the cops."

"Where did you learn moves like that?" Kim admired. "You took the Drac out without even blinking."

"What did you call him?" Jennifer avoided touching the pallid flesh again, but the youth's unconscious form filled her with an uncomfortable fascination.

"He's a Drac addict. They both are. The skin. The teeth. Like fangs. We were lucky. Drac's the foulest habit of them all."

"What do you mean?"

"It's a new drug," Kim supplied. "Hasn't been on the streets long but it's already making its mark. They say it gives you the greatest rush you can imagine, makes you feel like you're a god, immortal, all-powerful, like there's nothing you can't do, nothing you can't be. Trouble is, the high comes with a low, and the low's not good. You get addicted to Drac and you've signed up for your coffin. It changes you, see? Turns you into that." She gestured at the pale body with disgust. "And there's no way back. These guys weren't muggers after our money, Jen. They were after our blood, and I mean literally."

Jennifer looked up, horrified.

"It's like I said, Jen," Kim urged. "You don't know what's been happening around here. Just leave now and don't look back."

Leave now, her oldest friend had said. But how could she do that? *Don't look back.* How could she not? The blood of her family was on her conscience. It had to be avenged.

Under the glittering moon, through sordid, silent streets Jennifer picked her way home. Only it wasn't home now at all, was it; hadn't been since That Night. Their apartment had been left empty. Understandably, nobody really wanted to live and sleep in rooms where murder had been done. The whole place seemed blighted, stained. People had moved away, even the Tangs, even old Mrs. Koerner. And nobody had moved in, not even squatters.

As Jennifer wearily entered her apartment, she knew that but for her the building was deserted.

Only it wasn't.

Jennifer tensed among liquid shadows. Someone was there. Hearing sharpened by Spy High's aural enhancement program detected soft breathing, quiet movement. She wanted to scream but didn't.

From out of the darkness, a hand reached toward her.